"You Can Handle A *Baby* For A Few Minutes, Can't You?"

Hell, Jeff thought. He could hardly handle being in the same room with *Laura!* Her cheeks were flushed from the warm, moist air, tendrils of brown hair curled softly around her face, and her eyes looked dewy, despite the spark of challenge she was shooting at him.

His insides twisted with an unexpected pang. Obviously, he thought in disgust, his attraction for her hadn't weakened any, despite his hopes.

Only one week ago he was a perfectly contented man. His life and career were running smoothly. Now everything around him was in turmoil.

All because of one small person. And her irresistible nanny.

Don't miss the next installment of the irresistible BACHELOR BATTALION, *The Oldest Living Married Virgin,* coming in November, only in Silhouette Desire.

D1008036

Dear Reader,

The perfect treat for cool autumn days are nights curled up with a warm, toasty Silhouette Desire novel!

So, be prepared to get swept away by superstar Rebecca Brandewyne's MAN OF THE MONTH, *The Lioness Tamer,* a story of a magnetic corporate giant who takes on a *real* challenge—taming a wild virginal beauty. THE RULEBREAKERS, talented author Leanne Banks's miniseries about three undeniably sexy hunks—a millionaire, a bad boy, a protector—continues with *The Lone Rider Takes a Bride,* when an irresistible rebel introduces passion to a straight-and-narrow lady…and she unexpectedly introduces him to everlasting love. *The Paternity Factor* by Caroline Cross tells the poignant story of a woman who proves her secret love for a brooding man by caring for the baby she *thinks* is his.

Also this month, Desire launches OUTLAW HEARTS, a brand-new miniseries by Cindy Gerard about strong-minded outlaw brothers who can't stop love from stealing their own hearts, in *The Outlaw's Wife.* Maureen Child's gripping miniseries, THE BACHELOR BATTALION, brings readers another sensual, emotional read with *The Non-Commissioned Baby.* And Silhouette has discovered another fantastic talent in debut author Shirley Rogers, one of our WOMEN TO WATCH, with her adorable *Cowboys, Babies and Shotgun Vows.*

Once again, Silhouette Desire offers unforgettable romance by some of the most beloved and gifted authors in the genre. Don't forget to come back next month for more happily-ever-afters!

Regards,

Joan Marlow Golan
Senior Editor, Silhouette Desire

Please address questions and book requests to:
Silhouette Reader Service
U.S.: 3010 Walden Ave., P.O. Box 1325, Buffalo, NY 14269
Canadian: P.O. Box 609, Fort Erie, Ont. L2A 5X3

MAUREEN CHILD
THE NON-
COMMISSIONED BABY

SILHOUETTE *Desire*®
Published by Silhouette Books
America's Publisher of Contemporary Romance

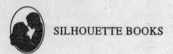

SILHOUETTE BOOKS

ISBN 0-373-76174-0

THE NON-COMMISSIONED BABY

Printed in U.S.A.

Books by Maureen Child

Silhouette Desire

Have Bride, Need Groom #1059
The Surprise Christmas Bride #1112
Maternity Bride #1138
*The Littlest Marine #1167
* *The Non-Commissioned Baby* #1174

* Bachelor Battalion

MAUREEN CHILD

was born and raised in southern California and is the only person she knows who longs for an occasional change of season. She is delighted to be writing for Silhouette and is especially excited to be a part of the Desire line.

An avid reader, she looks forward to those rare rainy California days when she can curl up and sink into a good book. Or two. When she isn't busy writing, she and her husband of twenty-five years like to travel, leaving their two grown children in charge of the neurotic golden retriever who is the *real* head of the household. She is also an award-winning historical writer under the names Kathleen Kane and Ann Carberry.

For Jaime and Kirk Brogdon
with love to celebrate Hayden.
A baby is a wonderful gift.
Enjoy every minute of your little miracle.

One

"Damn cats." Jeff Ryan muttered and swung both legs off the edge of the mattress. Stumbling across his bedroom in the heavily draped darkness, he slammed his big toe into the leg of a chair.

He jerked his foot up, cursed viciously, grabbed the throbbing toe and hopped to the closed door. Yanking it open, he let go of his foot and hobbled across the living room, wincing at the jagged slices of sunlight slanting through the half-opened blinds.

What was wrong with people? he thought. Why couldn't they keep their blasted cats at home instead of letting them sit outside his door howling like lost souls on the way to Hell?

Well, he'd had enough. This time, he'd catch the little beast and carry it straight to the manager's apartment—or the pound.

In a foul mood that was getting worse by the second, Jeff slid back the dead bolt, threw open the door and made a lunge for the cat.

One small problem.

That was no cat screaming from its roost in the basket just outside his door.

"A *baby?*"

At least, he told himself as he stared down in horror at the red-faced, screaming mass of humanity, he *thought* it was a baby. At the moment, it more resembled something out of *Aliens*.

What was going on around here? He looked up and down the length of the short hallway as if he expected to find the culprit who'd abandoned a baby like something out of a 1930s movie. But no one was there.

He looked down at the baby again, still stunned to find it on his doorstep.

Fat little arms and legs swung wildly in the air, while chubby hands grabbed for something that wasn't there. And the baby's howl was designed to puncture eardrums.

"Hey, kid," he said, bending down to jiggle the basket awkwardly. "Stick a sock in it, will you?"

The infant snorted, sniffed, looked at him, took a deep breath and screamed again.

And people wondered why he had never wanted kids.

Scowling in disgust, Jeff looked up and down the third floor's long hallway again. Not a sign of anybody. Wouldn't you know it? Where were his nosy neighbors when he really needed them? Sure, at eleven o'clock in the morning, no one was around. But let him come home at 2:00 a.m. with his date for the evening, and at the very least, old Mrs. Butler would have her head poked out her open door.

Glancing back at the Scream Machine, he noticed an envelope jutting up from the side of the basket, half-covered by a brightly colored knitted blanket.

Despite the thread of worry that had suddenly erupted in his bloodstream, Jeff reached down and plucked the envelope free. Slowly, dreading what he would find, he turned it over.

He cursed again, louder this time, as his gaze locked on his own name scrawled across the front of the envelope.

Captain Jeffrey Ryan, United States Marine Corps.

A baby on the doorstep? Things like that didn't really happen, did they? His fingers suddenly clumsy, he tore at the sealed flap and pulled out the folded papers. Smoothing them out, he read the note first.

Captain Ryan—Sorry to just leave the baby like this, but you weren't answering your door and I've got 45 minutes to catch a transport to Guam.

He paused. A fellow *Marine* had done this to him?

I volunteered to bring you the baby. The Sarge's will is enclosed, too, just so's everything's legal. A shame about the Sarge, but we all know you'll do right by his kid. Signed, Corporal Stanley Hubrick.

The Sarge? Jeff wondered. Sergeant who? And what did Corporal Hubrick mean, he knew Jeff would do right by the kid?

Head pounding from the baby's continued screeching, he skimmed the will once, then again, hitting only a few, significant words. Horrified, he lowered the papers and stared accusingly at the infant.

"No offense, kid, but I am *nobody's* guardian."

Ten minutes later, Jeff was on the phone, the receiver tucked between his ear and his shoulder as he rocked the incredibly unhappy baby in his arms.

At least it had stopped screeching. For the moment.

"I can't believe this," his sister repeated for the fifth time.

"You already said that."

"You're the baby's guardian?"

"According to this will, yes."

"Amazing."

"Peggy," he tried to reason with his sister, "you don't understand. I can't do this. What do I know about kids?"

"I don't know nothin' 'bout birthin' no babies, Miss Scarlett!" she said.

He inhaled sharply and gritted his teeth as she laughed.

"Very funny," he snarled a moment later, the humor in the situation completely escaping him. "Now, are you going to come down here and help me or not?"

"Not," Peggy said, amusement still touching the tone of her voice.

"Peg—" He stared, horrified as the baby started chewing on the sleeve of his T-shirt. Drool ran down the baby's cheeks and chin, pooling in the white fabric. "That's disgusting," he muttered.

"What?"

Snapping back to the bigger problem, he said, "Never mind. Peg, you've got to come."

"I always said you'd make a great father."

Yes, she had, but she had been the *only* one to think so.

"Cut it out." Silently, he shouted at his long-dead parents for gifting his sister with such a warped sense of humor. "This is serious. I've got to see about correcting this mess. Fast."

"What's to correct?" she said, and in the background, he heard one of his nephews apparently trying to behead his niece.

Jeff winced. Maybe he'd called the wrong person for advice on kids.

Her hand obviously half over the phone, Peggy calmly said, "Teddy, don't twist your sister's arm, you'll break it."

Unbelievable. Teddy. A nine-year-old enforcer.

"Honestly, Jeff," Peggy spoke to him again. "You're just going to have to deal with this. Whose baby is it, anyway?"

The name would be forever etched into his memory. "Sergeant Hank Powell. We served together in the Gulf. According to the note, Hank and his wife were killed in a car accident."

"Oh," soft-hearted Peggy sighed. "How terrible."

"Yeah," Jeff muttered, with a glance at the infant staring at him through wide blue eyes. Heck, he hadn't seen Hank in years. What had Jeff ever done to make the man hate him enough to saddle him with his kid?

"Oops," his sister said abruptly. "Gotta run.

Thomas's violin lesson is in fifteen minutes. Then Tina has ballet and Teddy has—''

"Karate?"

She laughed. "No, what am I, nuts? Drums."

Good Lord. Then, realizing she was hanging up on him, he panicked. "Peg, I need help. At least until I can figure out how to get out of this."

His sister sighed dramatically. After a moment, though, she perked right up. "Of course!" she said. "I'll call Laura."

"Laura?" he repeated. "Laura who?"

"I don't know why I didn't think of her right away," Peg went on, mostly to herself. "I'm sure she'd be willing."

"Willing to what?"

"Really, Jeff," Peggy said abruptly. "I've got to rush. Call you later to tell you when to expect Laura."

"Laura who?" he demanded again.

A dial tone hummed in his ear.

Abandoned, Jeff replaced the receiver and looked down at the finally quiet baby cradled against his side. Actually, when it was silent, holding it wasn't an entirely unpleasant sensation. A peaceful expression crossed the infant's face, and Jeff breathed a sigh of relief. Maybe the worst was over.

A moment later, he frowned at the sudden, damp warmth spreading down his hip and thigh. Realization dawned. He held the baby out at arm's length and stared down at his military green boxers.

Soaked.

In a much more disgusting manner than his T-shirt sleeve.

Slowly, he swiveled his appalled gaze to the baby. It laughed at him.

Judging from the screams coming from the other side of the door, Peggy's brother had his hands full. Laura Morgan winced slightly as the baby's wail hit a particularly high note.

She forced herself not to reach for that doorknob. Every instinct she possessed told her to go inside, pick up that baby and comfort it. But she had to be sure before she did any such thing.

Laura laughed at herself. A little late for rethinking. If she hadn't been sure, would she have taken a commuter flight from Santa Barbara to San Diego almost immediately after talking to Peggy? Would she even now be standing outside Captain Jeff Ryan's apartment, her life neatly packed into three battered suitcases?

Okay, fine. So she wanted the job. So it had seemed like a gift from the gods the minute Peggy had mentioned it. Laura loved babies. Had always planned on having several of her own by now. She frowned slightly. The best-laid plans, et cetera.

Now here she was, thirty years old, single and hoping that her best friend's brother would hire her for the summer. Because the only way she could ease the baby fever still holding her in its grip was with other people's children. There were no husband and kids in her future. All of those dreams had died with Bill eight years ago.

Well, that's a good start on the summer, she told herself. Drown yourself in a tidal wave of self-pity.

Always a great party favor. Designed to win friends and influence people.

"Psst!"

Laura frowned and looked to her right, but she didn't see anyone.

"Psst!" The voice was a little louder this time.

Studying the hall carefully, Laura finally spotted one of the apartment doors opened no more than half an inch. Staring at her through that narrow gap was one bright blue eye.

"Are you talking to me?" Laura asked hesitantly.

The door opened a hairbreadth wider, displaying a bit of the face that eye belonged to. A woman. Small, birdlike features, lined and etched by time, topped by wispy, snow white hair. "Are you going in there?" the woman asked.

"Yes," Laura answered with what she hoped was a friendly smile. Maybe the woman was too afraid to step into the hallway. But heck, the nightly news was enough to terrify Laura, for that matter. "I'm here to look after the baby."

"You look after yourself, missy," the woman said softly. "That one in there, he's a ladies' man."

"Is he really?" Laura turned a speculative eye on the door from behind which she could still hear the baby's cries.

"You don't look his usual type," the woman continued. "But I thought you should be told. Forewarned is forearmed, you know."

With that intriguing statement, she closed her door. In quick succession, Laura heard four locks slam home.

Interesting start to a new job, she thought. Yet she couldn't help wondering what Captain Ryan's type *was.*

Then she dismissed the old woman's warnings, steeled herself and lifted her right hand to knock. She stopped short when she heard a man shouting to be heard over the baby.

"Yeah?" he asked. "If Laura Morgan's so great, why isn't she here yet? I had to take the baby to the grocery store! And it wasn't pretty!"

Laura drew her head back and stared at the closed door as if she could see through the heavy wood to the angry man inside.

"Peggy," he shouted, "this isn't *funny.*"

Laura had to smile. Peggy Cummings's sense of humor was one of the things she liked best about her.

"I need help," he said. "Where the hell is this friend of yours, anyway?"

That cue was just too good to pass up. Quickly, she rapped her knuckles against the door.

It opened immediately.

The harried-looking man clutching a cordless phone to his ear stared at her. Well, he didn't match the description given to her by his sister. Peg had described her brother as "gorgeous, meticulously neat and with enough self-confidence for three healthy people."

The man in front of Laura now, though, looked wild. Short hair standing almost on end, he wore a white T-shirt stained with several different types of baby food, and a wet patch on his sharply creased trousers, which clung to his thigh. Bare feet only added to the image of a man on the edge.

None of that did a thing to take away from his good looks, though. His sharply defined features, strong jaw, straight nose and slightly full lips worked together to form a man too handsome for his own good. Peggy hadn't lied. He *was* gorgeous. Yet it wasn't only his face that was attractive. There was a strength about him that seemed to call to her. A knot of warmth uncurled in her stomach, sending ribbons of awareness spiraling through her limbs.

She breathed deeply, shifting her gaze to his eyes. A pale, icy blue, they seemed to look straight into her soul, poking and prodding to discover her secrets.

Laura shook her head slightly and looked away from his even stare deliberately. One thing she certainly *didn't* need was to start getting fanciful.

"I think she's here," he said into the phone. "Call me later."

He punched the disconnect button and set the phone down on a small table near the door.

"Are *you* Laura?" he asked, his blue-eyed gaze sweeping up and down her body in a flat second.

Instinctively, she stiffened, forgetting all about that instant, momentary bolt of attraction. Straightening her shoulders, she lifted her chin slightly. She had to do that anyway, to look him in the eye, but she hoped that the action looked defiant to him. Laura knew exactly what he was seeing when he stared at her.

A thirty-year-old woman, no makeup, wide brown eyes, dust brown hair pulled back into a ponytail. She wore comfortable penny loafers, baggy jeans and an oversize sweatshirt that proclaimed Ain't Life Grand? across the front.

Not very impressive, maybe. And as his neighbor had pointed out, probably not his type at all. But at least *she* could take care of a baby without looking as though she'd waded bare-handed through a war zone.

"Yes," she answered stiffly, giving him the same slow once-over that he had given her. "Jeff Ryan?"

He nodded abruptly, stepped past her into the hall and grabbed up her suitcases. Dropping them next to the wall, he closed the front door, then faced her.

"Where the heck have you been?" he demanded. "I expected you a half an hour ago."

She winced against the blare of the TV combining with the baby's cries. Pitching her voice a bit louder than normal, she snapped, "The plane was delayed."

Before he could comment on that, Laura sailed past Jeff Ryan into the unbelievably messy apartment. She paused long enough to turn off the TV, then followed the baby's screams to a basket set on the floor. Inside that straw-colored wicker bed, the infant lay on a handmade quilt, its chubby arms and legs pumping madly against the air.

Laura's heart melted.

Forgetting all about the man coming up behind her, she bent down, scooped up the baby and cradled it close to her chest. "It's all right, sweetie," she murmured as she rocked slowly back and forth, her right hand smoothing up and down the baby's back. "You're all right now. Laura's got you."

The screaming stopped.

The baby relaxed against her, its tiny body trembling as it sniffed and hiccuped.

"That's amazing," Jeff said softly, clearly afraid to

break whatever spell Laura had woven around the child.

"Not really," she said, sparing him a quick sidelong look. "A little comfort goes a long way."

He pushed one hand through the little bit of hair allowed by military regulations and shook his head as he looked over the wreckage of his living room.

"I could use a little comfort myself," he admitted. "She hasn't been that quiet all day."

A girl.

"What's her name?"

"According to the papers, it's Miranda. Miranda Powell."

"Well, hello, Miranda Powell," Laura whispered. She kissed the little head that was nestled just beneath her chin.

The baby's fingers tugged at the material of her sweatshirt, but Laura felt the small pulls all the way to her heart.

Jeff collapsed onto the cluttered sofa, then winced, lifted one hip and reached beneath him to pull a half-empty baby bottle out of his way. Tossing it onto the floor with a fatalistic shrug, he turned his gaze back to Laura. "You're not what I expected," he said.

She was rarely what anyone expected and had long ago ceased to care. But she was already in love with this baby. Laura wanted the job enough to remain pleasant as she asked, "Really, why?"

He shrugged, his gaze running over her carelessly. "Peg said you're a teacher, but you look like a kid yourself."

Translation, she thought, *short*. It was hardly her

fault that there were no tall genes in her family. "I'm thirty years old and a kindergarten teacher," she told him. "I have references if you'd like proof."

He held up one hand and shook his head. "Peggy's word is good enough for me. Besides—" he waved one hand to encompass the destruction around him "—as you can see, I'm in no position to quibble. I need help with her until I can figure out what to do about her."

One light brown eyebrow lifted. Laura felt it go up and tried to stop it, but she couldn't. What was there to figure out? she wanted to ask. There was only one thing to do with a baby.

Love it.

He must have read her expression because one corner of his mouth lifted slightly. She didn't want to notice what exceptional things even a hint of a smile did to his already handsome features. But she did.

"So," he asked, "you still want the job?"

She shouldn't. That sizzle of awareness she had experienced the second she laid eyes on him was not a good sign. But Laura couldn't have said no even if she wanted to. Not with Miranda's warm little body cuddled so closely.

"Yes."

"You understand that it may be for the entire summer?" he asked. "I mean, if I can handle everything right, the baby shouldn't be here more than a month or so. But you never know."

Any interest Laura might have had in him dissolved at his obvious haste to rid himself of the baby. Which was just as well anyway. She had already had her shot at love—and she'd lost. Besides, she could never be attracted to a man who so obviously didn't like children. Still, she wondered, what kind of man could turn his back on something so tiny? So defenseless?

"I understand perfectly," she said, and watched him give a satisfied nod.

"Good." He pushed himself up from the couch. "We can talk about salary tonight, if that's all right with you. My rules are simple. *You* take care of the baby. Agreed?"

"Agreed," she said.

He gave her a quick nod and started past her toward one of the closed doors on the other side of the room. He stopped dead in his tracks, though, when she said, "Hold on a minute, Captain. Now it's time for *you* to hear *my* rules."

Two

Jeff turned around slowly to face her.

All he really wanted was a shower, a nap and a change of clothes. Marine Corps boot camp hadn't been as rough on him as that one small baby girl had been. And yet, he thought as he looked into a pair of suddenly remote brown eyes, he had a feeling that his troubles were just beginning.

"Your rules?" he asked, determined to keep the upper hand in whatever argument was beginning to erupt. "Since when do employees make the rules?"

"Since now," she declared firmly.

Jeff rubbed the back of his neck. He should have known it wouldn't be easy. Any friend of his sister's was bound to be stubborn and independent as hell. He stared into those soft brown eyes of hers again and felt a stirring deep within him. Despite the fact that she was dressed like a refugee from the Goodwill, Jeff found himself wondering what her legs looked like when they weren't being hidden by seemingly *miles* of denim fabric.

Why would she dress like such a frump? What was she hiding from?

And why did he care?

He didn't, Jeff told himself. He couldn't afford to feel the sense of awareness already creeping through him. Laura Morgan was going to be living in his house, taking care of that baby. He wasn't about to mess that up by allowing his hormones to do his thinking for him.

Still, he told himself, he must be lonelier than he had thought, to be intrigued by a tiny woman dressed in clothes two sizes too big for her.

The look in her eyes as he continued to stare at her only grew frostier. So much for her sweatshirt, he smirked inwardly. He'd be willing to bet that she hadn't found anything "grand" about life in years.

But, since the baby was cooing contentedly, he was willing to put up with the poor man's Mary Poppins. As for his hormones—apparently, he needed to spend some time with one or two lady friends. That should take care of any bizarre interest in Laura Morgan.

"Okay," he said at last, folding his arms across his chest and completely ignoring the sticky substances on his T-shirt. "What are these *rules?*"

She nodded. "I'll stay here and take care of the baby for the summer, but..."

"Yeah?"

She inhaled sharply and tried to draw herself up to

a formidable height. He could have told her it was a futile attempt. She couldn't be more than five foot one. And that was no one's idea of intimidating.

"You're not hiring me to be your housekeeper." She paused for a look around at the mess his apartment had become. *"Or,"* she added, "your cook and laundress."

Insulted, Jeff tried to defend himself. "Look, until this morning, everything was under control—"

"Also," she said, cutting him off neatly, "there will be no walking around naked, no women strolling in and out of the apartment—"

"What are you—?"

"One of your neighbors thought it prudent to warn me about the fact that you're what she calls a 'ladies' man.'"

He shook his head and gave a resigned sigh. "Let me guess. White hair, big blue eyes?"

She nodded, but he thought he saw the ghost of a smile twitching at her lips.

"Agnes Butler," he said, the elderly woman's features forming in his mind. "For lack of anything better to do, she spies on me."

Twin brown eyebrows arched high on her forehead. "Spying? Sounds a little paranoid."

Briefly, he recalled all the times he had strolled down that short hallway and spotted his neighbor, her eye glued to a partially opened door. Yeah, *spying* was the right word.

"You're not paranoid," he told her, "if they really *are* after you."

A moment or two of silence passed. At last, she

nodded and said, "Yes, well, the rest of the rules are pretty simple."

"There's more?" he asked.

She smiled. "No foul language—"

"Now, just a minute—" he said, trying to interrupt, but she was on a roll.

"No talking before coffee in the morning, and no loud TV or radio after eleven at night."

Jeff stared at her. Was she finished? Or just pausing for breath? A few seconds ticked by, and he told himself that apparently, she'd reached the end of her demands. Well, fine. Now it was *his* turn.

He would tell her just what she could do with her rules. This was *his* house after all. Where did she get off telling him when he could or couldn't watch *his* TV? And what about women? So he didn't exactly have a parade of females trooping in and out of his apartment every day and night. If he *wanted* to, he wasn't going to be stopped by her.

"Listen up, lady," he started, "I don't know who the hell you think you are…"

She froze, stiffening for a fight.

Miranda sniffled, shifting against a suddenly tense body.

Recognizing the signs of baby distress already, Jeff lowered his voice and spoke in a quiet, reasonable tone. "You can't order me around. *I'm* the employer here, you know."

"I can tell you what I expect," Laura countered, her voice matching his. "And if you don't like it, you can find someone else."

He didn't believe the threat. Even as she said it, her

arms were tightening around the baby as if afraid that he would try to take Miranda from her forcibly.

No worries there.

But with the position he was in, he couldn't afford to take the risk. If she left, he'd be right back where he started that morning. In deep trouble, begging Peggy for help.

All right, he could swallow a little bit of pride for the sake of his sanity. And he could even learn to deal with her ridiculous rules. *Anything* to keep her here and the baby quiet. After all, it wasn't forever. Just for the summer. By the end of three months, he would either have found a suitable replacement guardian for the baby or, God help him, a permanent nanny to help him raise Hank Powell's kid.

Abruptly, he said, "Fine. Agreed."

"Thank you." She accepted his defeat gracefully. "But as long as we're discussing this situation, I should like to add one more rule to my list."

He snorted disbelievingly. "What's left?"

"I'd like to state clearly right from the first," she said, "that I am *not* interested in you romantically, so I would appreciate it very much if you would keep your distance."

Jeff laughed, the first good laugh he'd had all morning. Pointedly running his gaze over her slowly, he shook his head and said, "No problem."

Once Jeff was out of the shower—and Laura had even resorted to turning on the TV so she wouldn't have to listen to the spray of water and imagine it pummeling his naked, no doubt gorgeous body—they set things to rights.

The living room was a disaster.

With a fed and changed Miranda watching happily from her wicker basket, Laura and Jeff worked together to rebuild the place. So much for her rule about not being a housekeeper. As most of the clutter was cleared away, she noticed that the apartment wasn't exactly homey. In fact, it was surprisingly impersonal.

A sprinkling of framed photos and commendations hung on the beige walls, but there were no paintings. Tweed fabric covered the couch and two chairs that sat on the tan wall-to-wall carpeting. There was an impressive stereo system and a large-screen TV on one wall, and a fireplace that looked as though it had never been used stood on the opposite wall. A two-person table sat at the end of the kitchen, and there were two bedrooms, one on either side of the single bathroom.

She tried not to think about having to share that bathroom with Jeff Ryan for the next three months. Luckily for her, she no longer noticed things like just how good-looking Jeff Ryan was. If she had been the slightest bit interested in finding a man, these next few months could have been torture.

Of course, she had thought she was past noticing the fresh, clean scent of a man's aftershave, too.

"So," he said, and snapped her attention to him. He folded up yet another brown paper grocery bag as he asked, "How come a kindergarten teacher didn't already have a summer job nailed down?"

She stacked the last can of formula in what had been an empty cabinet, then closed the door and straightened up. "I did," she admitted. "This one sounded like more fun."

He snorted a laugh. "More fun than what?"

"Transferring card catalogs to computer in the local library."

He whistled low and long. "You're right, not fun." He glanced at the baby a few feet away. "But this is?"

"Sure."

"Lady, you've got a strange sense of fun."

Peggy had told Laura that Jeff not only had no experience taking care of children, but also that he didn't even like them.

She frowned at him. "Your sister has three kids. Don't you remember how cute they were when they were little?"

He shrugged and bent down to neatly place the folded bags in the appropriate rack just inside the pantry door. "I remember they cried. A lot," he said as he stood up again and closed the door. "They smelled bad and they couldn't even talk to tell you *why* they cried all the time."

"No wonder you never visit Peggy and her family."

He looked at her. "Is that what she said?"

Was he offended? How could he be? "It's true, isn't it? You see them about once a year?"

"Yeah, it's true." He folded his arms across his chest and leaned one hip against the blond wood countertop. "She tell you why?"

"She said you're uncomfortable around kids." Laura didn't tell him the rest. Did he really need to know that his own sister, though she loved him, thought he was too self-involved to be concerned about family?

"That's part of it," he admitted, letting his gaze slide from Laura to the baby, now chewing contentedly on her own fist. "But mostly it's because I can't even talk to Peggy and her husband anymore."

"Why not?" Laura asked. Peggy and Jim Cummings were two of the nicest people she'd ever known. Was the woman's own brother too dense to see that?

He shook his head and smiled without humor. "Before they had those kids, Peggy and Jim and I had some good times. Skiing, sailing, took a few trips together."

"And?" she prodded, interested now.

"And, the minute the first kid was born, it was all over." He pushed away from the counter, walked across the utilitarian kitchen and stood, staring down at the baby in the basket. "They became *parents* in the worst possible sense. All they talked about was Thomas. His teeth. His upset stomach. His first steps. The first time he used a spoon by himself, you would have thought he was Einstein reincarnated."

Laura smiled to herself as she stared at Jeff's broad back. His sister was *still* like that. Just a few weeks ago, Peggy had called to crow over Tina winning the second-grade spelling bee.

Like any other good parent would.

"But that's perfectly natural," Laura said, and walked to stand beside him. Looking down at Miranda, she smiled. "They're proud of their children."

"They're boring," he countered, swiveling his head

to stare at her. "They used to have plans. Ambitions. Now those ambitions are all for the kids."

An emotion she couldn't quite identify flickered in his pale blue eyes briefly, then disappeared. "All parents want good things for their kids," she said quietly.

"Sure," he countered. "But do they have to stop being people themselves to be good parents?"

"Peggy and Jim are *terrific* people," she argued, defending her friends.

He shook his head as he looked at her. Once again, Laura felt a flutter of awareness dance through her bloodstream. Deliberately, she squashed it.

"Is it so wrong to have ambitions and dreams for your kids?" she asked, determined to keep this conversation going, if only to keep her mind too busy to daydream.

He thought about her question for a long minute, then shrugged. "Not for Peggy and Jim," he said, shifting his gaze back to the baby, now intently staring up at the two adults. "But that's not me," he continued. "I have plans for my career. Plans I've worked toward long and hard."

"Everybody makes plans," she said.

It was as if he hadn't heard her.

"I'm going to be the youngest general in the corps," he stated. Then he glanced at the wicker basket. "And I'm not going to let *anything* stop me."

Three

A nightmare.

In less than twelve hours, his life had become a waking nightmare.

Jeff stumbled across the living room, stepped on a fallen pacifier and grunted as the dull yet stabbing pain lanced from his arch straight up his leg.

"Are you all right?" Laura asked, her voice high enough to carry over the baby's wailing.

"Dandy," he muttered, then flopped down beside her on the couch. Instantly, he lifted one hip and pulled a leaking baby bottle from under his butt. "How can one kid need so much *stuff?*" he grumbled to no one in particular as he slammed the plastic bottle down onto the coffee table.

Laura had only one lamp on, and in the dim light,

he surveyed what had, only that morning, been his sanctuary.

Blankets, clean diapers, bottles, pacifiers, lotion, powder—there was enough junk in the already small room to satisfy a battalion of babies. So why wasn't the only baby present happy?

"Why is she screaming like that?" he demanded.

"I think she's teething," Laura said, and hitched Miranda higher on her shoulder.

"Perfect," he said. "How long does *that* last?"

In the soft light, Laura smirked at him. "According to my watch, she should be finished in another three and a half minutes."

His eyebrows lifted. He knew sarcasm when he heard it, and if he wasn't so damn tired, he might have taken a shot himself. As it was, his heart just wasn't in it.

Laura whispered to the baby while stroking the infant's back in long, gentle motions. Jeff watched her, at first for lack of anything else to do, but after a moment, because he couldn't seem to look away.

And he also couldn't figure out why. That nightgown of hers certainly wasn't alluring. An oversized T-shirt emblazoned Life Is A Trip, Don't Miss It hung to midthigh. Although, he thought, the surprisingly shapely legs revealed by that shirt were not bad at all. As he watched, she shifted slightly, tugging the hem down fruitlessly.

Her thick brown hair lay loose on her shoulders, and he had to admit that the casual style complemented her features far better than the scraped-back ponytail she'd worn earlier. Her high cheekbones were more sharply defined in the soft light. Light brown eyebrows arched high over eyes that looked as deep and mysterious as a moonless night. Her generous mouth was curved in a half smile even as the baby in her arms flailed tiny fists against her face. Laura merely caught one of those fists, opened it and kissed the small, chubby palm.

His jaw tightened, and something inside him twisted. A curl of desire trickled through him, and he deliberately squashed it. Shifting position on the sofa, he wished he had taken the time to grab his robe before leaving his room. Wearing only a pair of boxer shorts, Jeff felt suddenly, decidedly uncomfortable.

He was staring.

In the shadowy light, Laura saw his pale blue eyes darken as he watched her. Her gaze slid away, unfortunately dropping to his bare, muscular chest. Her heart beat faster, and her palms were damp. Breath after breath straggled into her lungs even as she told herself that she was probably just too warm in the overheated apartment.

All she needed was to turn the heater down.

This had nothing to do with how attractive he was. After all, she didn't even notice things like that anymore.

Laura's gaze flicked to his again, then quickly away. Her stomach fluttered and twitched. Why was he looking at her so strangely? She wasn't exactly a supermodel, so what did he find so fascinating that he couldn't stop watching her?

Miranda sucked in a gulp of air, coughed, choked, then cried again, pumping her little legs against Laura's chest. Immediately Laura dismissed Jeff Ryan and the strange things he did to her stomach and concentrated on the baby.

"It's all right, sweetheart," she soothed in a low, humming tone.

"No, it's not," Jeff said, his voice grumpy. "Is she ever going to shut up so I can get some sleep tonight?"

Laura frowned at him, furious at his impatience. Carefully, she shifted the baby to her lap and began to rock slowly. "Well, now that you've told her that she's disturbing you, I'm sure she'll settle right down," Laura snapped. "After all, how can the throbbing pain of new, sharp teeth slicing through her gums compare with your being tired?"

He scowled at her and sat forward, leaning his forearms on his thighs. "You know—" he started to say.

"Yes, I do," she cut him off neatly. "I know that you don't give a—" she broke off, searched for a word, then continued "—hoot about this baby. All you care about is yourself."

"Up until eleven this morning," he reminded her, "that's all I had to worry about."

"Well, things've changed."

"Tell me about it." He waved one hand at her and the baby. "In less than twenty-four hours, I've inherited a baby and a snotty nanny."

"Snotty?"

"Snotty," he repeated.

Bouncing the baby a little faster on her knee, Laura's rocking motion became a bit jerky. "You are the one who needed my help," she told him stiffly, still smarting from the "snotty" remark.

"Help," he clarified. "Not harassment."

"Now I'm harassing you?"

"What do you call it?" he asked hotly.

"I call it looking out for this baby when no one else seems willing."

Miranda sniffled and rubbed her eyes with both fists. Then, reaching down, she snatched at the hem of Laura's nightgown and lifted it. Jamming the fabric into her mouth, she chewed furiously.

"I didn't say I wasn't willing," he said.

"Of course you did," Laura countered, paying no attention to the suddenly quiet baby in her arms. "Not five minutes after I got here, you were talking about finding a way out of this situation."

A long silent moment passed, neither of them aware that Miranda had stopped screaming. Finally, Jeff stood up, and ran one hand across the top of his head. Something Laura had already noticed he did quite often when he was upset.

"Look," he said, gazing down at her in the half-light, "maybe we got off on the wrong foot."

"How's that?" She looked up at him, determined to keep her gaze locked on his face. Thankfully, she was immune to the distraction of a well-muscled chest, but there was no point in taking chances.

"I'm not some kind of monster," he told her, and his voice sounded distant, quiet. "I don't even *hate* kids."

Wow. A testimonial. Her hold on Miranda tightened protectively.

"It's just that I'm not..." He shook his head and

looked off into the shadowy corner of the room. "Hell, I'm nobody's idea of father material."

Was that a wistful tone in his voice? "You could be," she said hesitantly. "If you tried."

He snorted a choked laugh. "You're a lot more sure than I am, Mary Poppins," he commented.

Laura stood up, hitching the baby higher in her arms. Forcing herself to look into Jeff's eyes, she said, "I thought Marines weren't afraid of a challenge."

One corner of his mouth lifted in a sardonic half smile. She told herself that it was lucky for her she was beyond noticing things like the dimple he had in his right cheek.

"Challenges, no," he told her. "Slaughters, yes. And I have a feeling that kid's already got me outnumbered." Pausing, he listened for a minute, then said, "Hey, she's not crying anymore."

True, Laura thought. Miranda had finally settled down, and neither one of them had realized it.

Jeff looked at the baby in her arms, then pulled in a deep breath as his gaze slipped lower.

Laura saw his jaw tighten. Glancing down, she looked for whatever it was that had caused such a reaction in him. Her eyes widened immediately. The hem of her nightshirt was drawn up to just beneath her left breast. Exposed to Jeff's view was not only a wide expanse of flesh, but the electric blue lace bikini underwear she wore. Laura's one concession to femininity in her wardrobe had always been her secret weakness for beautiful lingerie.

Well, it wasn't a secret anymore.

"Oh, my goodness," she blurted as she tugged at the fabric even while turning her back on Jeff.

"Wow," he murmured.

Laura silently thanked heaven that it was so dark in the living room. She felt the heated flush of embarrassment rush to her cheeks and was relieved he wouldn't see it.

"Who would have thought you'd be hiding lace under all that camouflage you were wearing earlier?"

It would have been too much to hope for that he would ignore what he'd just seen. But did he *really* have to talk about it, too?

"I think it would be better if we just pretend this never happened," Laura said as she tugged at the fabric, hoping to restore her dignity. But the baby, happily chewing on the soft cotton, was blissfully unaware of Laura's predicament. Little fingers curled into the material and hung on with a surprisingly strong grip.

"Nothing *did* happen," Jeff stated.

Laura shot him a quick, furtive look over her shoulder. An odd gleam shone in his eyes, but she dismissed it as a trick of the low lighting. For whatever reason, he wasn't going to talk about her underwear anymore. That was enough.

"Good," she said quickly. "Now, if you'll excuse me," she grunted as she stepped around him, keeping her back to him at all times. "I think I'll put Miranda down. She seems contented enough now."

He chuckled.

She heard him, but since she still wasn't decently covered, she didn't turn around. "What's so funny?"

she demanded, stopping just outside her open bedroom door.

"Nothing," he said, his voice low and intimate. "It's just that I was thinking how alike Miranda and I are after all."

"What does that mean?" she asked, knowing even as she did so that it was a mistake.

"It means that pulling a woman's nightgown up always makes me pretty content, too."

She inhaled sharply. Straightening her shoulders, she ignored the deep chuckles coming from behind her and walked into her room. When the door was safely closed, Laura leaned back against it.

Miranda laughed, let go of the nightgown and patted Laura's cheeks.

"Oh, sure," she said to the smiling baby. "*Now* you cooperate."

Jeff cupped his head in his hands and inhaled the scent of the strong black coffee in front of him. His eyes felt like two marbles in a bucket of sand.

Between the baby's restless first night in his apartment and the heart-stopping peep show Laura had unwittingly given him, he had lain awake most of the night. Visions of blue lace and smooth, lightly tanned flesh had haunted him.

Even now, he could see her, flustered and embarrassed as she turned away from him. If the light in the room had been better, Jeff was willing to bet that he could have seen a blush steal across her cheeks.

How long had it been since he'd known a woman to blush?

He inhaled sharply, blew the air out of his lungs in a frustrated sigh and told himself that he would be in real bad shape if he was attracted to women like Laura Morgan.

Thankfully, he wasn't.

Give him a well-dressed, sophisticated career woman every time. The motherly type had never done a thing for him. Although, you really couldn't classify those blue lace bikini panties as *motherly*.

He groaned quietly.

Should have taken another sick day, he thought. A man just couldn't function on two hours' sleep. Unless of course, he thought as he leaned back in his chair, he was on a battlefield. Live ammunition whizzing past your head had a way of waking you right up.

"Captain?"

Jeff blinked groggily, almost surprised to find himself in his office. He looked at the younger man poking his head in the doorway. "What is it, Corporal Warren?"

"A Private Higgins is here, sir. Says he has those files you wanted."

"Send him in," Jeff ordered sharply. He'd been waiting all morning for these records to arrive.

A young, eager-looking redheaded kid in the standard camouflage utility uniform strode into his office. File folders tucked neatly beneath his left arm, the kid came to an abrupt stop in front of Jeff's desk and flashed a picture-perfect salute.

Nodding absentmindedly, Jeff reached for the files.

"This is all I could find, sir," the private said as he handed the manila folders over. "If you'd like, I could make a few calls, see if there's anything else available."

Jeff opened the files and glanced quickly over the pages inside. Then he looked up again. "That won't be necessary, Private. Thank you."

"Aye, sir." Another salute, an abrupt about-face and the kid was gone.

"Corporal Warren," Jeff called. His clerk appeared instantly.

"Sir?"

"Close my door, Corporal. No interruptions."

"Aye, sir."

In seconds, the door was closed and Jeff was alone. Picking up his coffee, he started reading all about the man who had given him Miranda. Not that he didn't remember him. But it had been more than five years since he'd seen the sergeant. And in the military, an officer served with so many men—sometimes names and faces blurred without a good prodding of the memory.

Twenty minutes later, Jeff sat back in his chair, flipping the file closed with the tips of his fingers. Setting his elbows on the arms of his chair, he steepled his fingers and stared at the windows opposite his desk.

Memories raced through his mind. Desert sun, mind-boggling heat and the constant adrenaline rush of impending battle. Days and nights spent in the company of men willing to die at a moment's notice.

Abruptly, he reached for his phone and the Rolodex on the corner of his desk. He flipped quickly through the cards until he'd found the one he wanted.

Punching in a phone number, he held the receiver to his ear, sat back again and waited.

Laura woke up instantly and lay perfectly still.

Even before her mind had assured her that everything was all right, she heard his voice, a hushed whisper in the darkness.

Turning her head on the pillow until she was facing the newly purchased crib against the far wall in her room, Laura saw Jeff, leaning his forearms on the top rail, staring down at the sleeping baby.

"I remember your father now, kiddo," he was saying, his voice oddly tight. "I called up his service records today."

The baby whimpered in her sleep, and Jeff reached down to awkwardly pat her. Laura smiled in the darkness.

"He was a good man, your dad," Jeff said. "Got a Bronze Star for bravery."

Miranda kicked her blankets off, and Jeff carefully replaced them.

A trickle of warmth moved through Laura. Maybe she had misjudged him. Maybe he cared more for the baby than even *he* knew.

Moonlight, peering through a part in the curtains, washed her otherwise dark room with a pale ivory cast. In the indistinct light, Jeff was no more than a shadow, yet she could read tension in every line of his body.

"We fought together, you know." He sighed heavily and shook his head, as if lost in the memories. "Hank kept me from making a damn fool of myself during my first battle. And I saved his sergeant's stripes for him when he came up against a major with more brass than brains.''

Laura held her breath, wanting to say something to him, to let him know that she wasn't asleep. But at the same time, she wanted him to go on. She wanted to know more about him.

She told herself that it was only because she was working for him and would be living in his house for the next three months.

But it was more than that, and she knew it.

Somehow, in the past twenty-four hours, he had forced some of the ice around her heart to melt. Why and how, she wasn't sure.

Maybe it was the helpless expression on his face when he looked at Miranda. And maybe it was what he did for a pair of boxer shorts.

She scowled to herself, disgusted at this turn of events. Laura didn't want to care about another man. She'd already found and lost the love of her life. What was the point of settling for second best?

"You had a good dad, Miranda," Jeff said quietly, bringing Laura's attention back to him. "I'll do my best to see to it you get a good one again." He reached into the crib and smoothed his palm gently across the top of the baby's head. "Good night, kiddo."

So much for her giving him the benefit of the doubt. All of her warm, fuzzy feelings for nothing. Apparently, he still had every intention of finding a way to squeak out of being Miranda's guardian.

Laura bit down hard on her bottom lip to keep from speaking. *How* could she possibly be attracted to a man who could so casually walk away from a baby entrusted to his care?

Her gaze followed him to the door and the slice of light spearing in from the living room. Laura ground her teeth together in frustration. She couldn't say anything. If she did, he would know that she had deliberately lain there eavesdropping.

"And good night to you, too, Laura," he added softly, just before leaving and closing the door behind him.

She sat straight up in bed.

Blast him. He had known the whole time that she was awake! He must be laughing himself sick right now, guessing what it had cost her to keep her mouth shut.

Well, he wouldn't laugh long. Whether he knew it or not, he had just given her permission to make a few comments on what he'd been telling Miranda.

Casting a quick look at the baby, Laura climbed out of bed and headed for the door. She paused briefly to snatch up her bathrobe and throw it on.

If they were going to talk, she'd make sure his mind was on what she was saying. *Not* on her underwear.

Four

In the kitchen, Jeff smiled to himself as Laura's bedroom door opened, then closed again softly. He'd known she wouldn't stay in her room. In fact, he'd been counting on it. For reasons he didn't want to explore at the moment, he wanted, no, *needed* to see her.

Picking up the chilled bottle of wine, he poured each of them a glass and was turning around to hand it to her when she walked in.

Surprised, she blinked and stopped dead.

Instantly, the taunting memory of blue lace bikinis withered and died along with his fantasies. Looking her over quickly, he wondered just how old that bathrobe was.

Faded pink terry cloth hung on her small frame with all the grace and dignity of a drunk clutching a light pole. The nubby fabric, rubbed smooth in places, was a patchwork of stains and tears. Long, loose threads waved lazily every time she moved, and the single front pocket looked stuffed with tissues and God knew what else.

"Nice robe," he commented wryly.

She tightened the threadbare sash around her waist and tossed her hair back behind her shoulders. One light eyebrow arched high on her forehead as she looked him up and down quickly. "Nice camouflage," she snapped. "Were you out hiding in the forest?"

He grinned. Ratty robe or not, he was glad to see her.

"You knew I was awake the whole time, didn't you?"

Her cheeks were flushed, and her hair looked soft and tousled, as if a man had spent hours running his fingers through it.

Jeff inhaled sharply. Better if he didn't let his mind wander too far down *that* road. Deliberately, he took another look at her worn robe before meeting her deep brown eyes. Those shadowy depths sparkled with impatience and suspicion as she watched him.

"Not the whole time," he said with a shrug, and held out one of the crystal wineglasses toward her. "Wine?"

She ignored the offer. "Why didn't you say something?"

"I was talking to Miranda," he said, wondering now why it was that he'd wanted to see her. "Do you want the wine or not?"

"Oh." She looked at the glass, then back to him. "I don't think so."

Still holding it toward her, he said, "It's only half a glass, Laura."

She thought about it for a moment longer, then reached out and took it from him. "All right. Thanks."

Inclining his head slightly, he said, "You're welcome." Taking his wine, he walked past her into the living room. A single lamp had been left on. The room lay mostly in darkness, with deeper shadows gathering in the corners.

Tossing his hat onto the coffee table, Jeff sat down on the couch, leaned his head against the high back and sighed heavily. Damn, it felt good to relax. He propped one foot on the edge of the table, and as proof of his tiredness, didn't move a muscle when Laura stepped over his extended leg to take a seat beside him on the sofa.

Turning his head slightly, he looked at her. She was watching him again, with that solemn stare he was already getting used to.

"Bad day?" she asked.

"Long day," he corrected.

Moments of sweet silence stretched out between them. After being surrounded by people and the noise and hustle at the base all day, Jeff had always craved the peace and quiet of a few minutes alone. Solitude helped him think. Gave him time to consider his past, his future.

He'd been alone for so many years, this small ritual was second nature to him. But tonight it was different.

Tonight there was someone else's breathing whispering into the darkness. Instead of absolute, undisturbed silence, he heard the hush of skin brushing against skin as she crossed her legs beneath her, Indian style. When she took a sip of her wine, the tiny clink of her front teeth hitting the crystal sounded out.

Surprising himself, Jeff found that he was actually enjoying sharing this moment of quiet with someone who valued peace enough to know not to talk.

It was...comforting in a way he hadn't expected.

"Was it true?" she asked softly.

Jeff smiled to himself. Apparently, Laura *could* be quiet. She simply preferred not to. "What?" he asked.

"Everything you said about Miranda's father?"

"Yeah." He nodded, took a drink of wine and sat higher on the couch, half turning to look at her.

"But you said yesterday that you didn't even remember him."

"I know." He reached up and rubbed one hand across his face. Jeff had read through Hank Powell's files three times. Each time, he had asked himself how he could have mentally misfiled the man.

The only answer he had come up with was one he was sure Laura wouldn't understand.

"I just don't get it," she said. Scooping one hand through her hair, she propped her elbow on the sofa back. "How can you forget a friend?"

Jeff shook his head. "I didn't say he was a friend."

"You said he saved you from making a fool of yourself."

He winced tightly. There was a memory he didn't particularly want to relive.

"He did," Jeff admitted, hoping she'd let it go at that. He should have known better.

"Then—"

"He wasn't my friend," Jeff interrupted. "He was my sergeant."

In the dim light, he saw her shake her head in confusion. Suddenly unable to sit still, he got up, walked to the nearest window and yanked on a nylon cord. The window blinds flew up with a loud clatter. When they were secured, Jeff set his wineglass down on the windowsill, leaned both palms on either side of it and stared through the glass at the town outside.

Bright splashes of neon decorated the night. Shimmers of primary colors reflected off the night sky. Convenience stores, gas stations, even the theater down the street added to the blazing clutter.

He stared at civilization's landmarks until they faded into a kaleidoscopic blur of light and color. Slowly, his mind replaced the familiar view with one he'd spent years trying to forget.

A sun-washed desert rose up in his memory. Men and machinery moving across endless miles of sand and heat under a sky so wide and empty it glittered in the noonday sun like a stainless steel skillet.

Hank Powell, a grizzled, tough, no-nonsense first sergeant, had had the guts to look a fresh, young, know-it-all lieutenant in the face and tell him he was wrong.

Jeff smiled slightly at the memory of what had been an embarrassing and infuriating moment. It had been hard enough admitting to himself that he didn't know what he was doing. But to have First Sergeant Powell call him on it was especially humbling. He'd made every effort since then to forget it.

"What happened?" Laura asked from behind him.

The desert slid back into the past where it belonged. Jeff half turned to look at her. "It was my first tour. I was young and stupid." He shook his head slowly. "But thankfully, not too stupid to learn. I made a mistake that could have gotten me and my men killed."

"What?" she asked, and he could see the curiosity stamped on her features.

"Doesn't matter now. All that matters is that Hank Powell stopped me in time." Picking up his wineglass, Jeff eased down onto the windowsill, perching on the edge as he faced her. Memories swelled around him. "Hank was the kind of Marine that would make John Wayne look like a sissy."

She gave him a tentative smile. "Sounds scary."

"You bet."

"You liked him."

He thought about that for a long minute. *Like* the first sergeant? "I admired the hell out of him," he finally said, and even then that wasn't really enough to explain the relationship. Jeff drained the rest of his wine, then twirled the empty glass between his fingers. "He taught me a lot."

"Yet you didn't remember him."

"I never actually said I didn't remember him. I knew the name." He shot her a sidelong glance. "I hadn't seen him in at least five years."

"Still…"

Jeff's grip on the fragile crystal tightened noticeably. He looked down at whitened knuckles and deliberately forced himself to relax his hold on the slender stem. Taking a deep, calming breath, he said, "I remember people fine, Laura." His voice sounded rough and thick, even to himself. "Every time I close my eyes, I see their faces clearly."

"Who?"

"The dead."

Laura sucked in a gulp of air. Even from across the room, she saw the shadows in his eyes. Instantly, her mind furnished images of what he must see. What he must recall about battles she had only read about from a safe, insulating distance.

She took a sip of wine, forcing the cool, smooth liquid past the sudden knot in her throat. Then she leaned forward and set the unfinished drink carefully down on the coffee table.

What could she say? She watched him for a long, quiet moment and knew he wasn't in the room with her anymore. His features shifted, tightened. Clearly, the memories, once unleashed, raced through his brain. Memories she had prodded him to relive.

Suddenly, she wanted to go to him, slip her arms around his shoulders and comfort him like she would a lost child.

But he was no boy.

And the feelings he stirred in her weren't entirely altruistic. *Or* motherly. In the soft glow of the single lamp, she saw the sharp, strong planes of his face as if in a dream. Her gaze drifted over him and locked on his hands. His long fingers toyed with the empty crystal glass, turning it this way and that, slowly, hypnotically.

She watched his fingers stroke the foggy glass, tracing the intricate pattern etched into the crystal. She wondered what it would feel like to be touched by hands as gentle as those. To be explored with the same finesse and care.

To be the woman he turned to when his dreams refused him sleep.

Her stomach fluttered uneasily, and her heartbeat quickened. One minute she was sympathizing with him, wanting to ease a years-old pain, and the next, she was caught up in sensual imagery that left her body throbbing with an ache she hadn't known possible.

Yet more disturbing than those sensations was the emotional ache he caused in her. She felt herself wanting to give. To soothe. To love.

Quickly, she took a mental step backward.

Closing her tired eyes, she hoped to rid herself of the fantasies building within her. It didn't work. As if in a dream, Jeff leaned over her, whispering her name. She arched toward him, lifting her arms in a welcoming embrace.

He held her close to his chest, and she listened to the steady, reassuring beat of his heart. In her drowsy, half-asleep state, she snuggled into him. "Where are we going?" she murmured.

"*You're* going," he said quietly. "To bed."

She tightened her arms around his neck and leaned her head back to look up at him. "You're dangerous, Captain."

He glanced down at her as he stopped outside her bedroom door. His arms tightened slightly around her.

"Me? I'm a Marine," he said. "One of the good guys."

She shook her head slowly, unsure if he was purposely misunderstanding her or not. Lifting one hand, she stroked her fingers along the line of his cheek and felt his jaw muscle tighten in response. Oh, yeah. He knew exactly what she was talking about.

"It wouldn't be a good idea," she told him.

"Probably not," he agreed, and turned his face into her touch.

"I'm not interested in a relationship, you know."

"Me, either," he said, his teeth nipping at the pads of her fingers.

Electrical charges skittered through her bloodstream.

"We'd regret it, Jeff."

"Maybe, Laura," he whispered. "But we'd never forget it."

Oh, good heavens, she thought. What had she gotten herself into?

Without another word, he opened the door, carried her into the darkness and crossed the room to her bed. As if she were the most delicate flower in the world, he laid her down on the mattress. Bracing his hands on either side of her head, he leaned in close and brushed a kiss across her lips.

Her heart stumbled, stopped, then started beating again, much quicker than before. Staring up at him, Laura, for the first time in years, couldn't think of a single thing to say.

Jeff straightened up slowly, whispered, "Sleep

well,'' then left the room as if the hounds of hell were on his heels.

Laura lay wide-awake in the darkness, listening to Miranda's baby noises and the wild, frantic beating of her own heart.

Hours later, muted sunshine drifted in through her bedroom curtains. Morning. Laura sat up, groaned and rubbed her eyes. No doubt about it—a person really did need more than one or two hours' sleep a night.

Helplessly, she shook her head. She was in deep trouble here. She'd only known Jeff Ryan a couple of days, and already he had begun to sneak past the barriers she had erected around her heart.

Suddenly, the three long months of summer stretched out ahead of her like an eternity. How would she ever survive living in such close quarters with the man?

That night over pizza, Jeff looked at the woman sitting across from him at the table. Hair scraped back into a high ponytail, no makeup and a lime green sweatshirt that read, Don't Sweat The Small Stuff, she was not the kind of woman dreams were built around.

So why, he wondered silently, did *his* dreams furnish her with a starring role? All night, he'd been haunted by the memory of her slight form cuddled in close to him. By the taste of her lips. By the soft sigh of her breath.

Good God—he was digging himself a trench here.

''Have you been looking into Miranda's guardianship papers?'' she asked suddenly.

Grateful to end his disturbing train of thought, he

nodded. She hadn't said one word about their little tryst in the darkness, and he was profoundly grateful for *that*, too.

"I talked to my lawyer yesterday," he admitted, remembering the call he'd made after reading Sergeant Powell's record.

"I've never known anyone who had their own lawyer," she said.

He shrugged. "He's actually the brother of one of the captains on base. We all go to him with legal questions."

"And what was your question?"

Jeff picked up a slice of pepperoni-and-mushroom pizza, then set it back down again. Almost guiltily, he glanced at Miranda, her little face covered with a layer of strained green beans. "I told him about how I found her and explained the note and the will that was with her."

"And?"

He leaned back in his chair, his appetite suddenly gone. "And, though he says the means of delivering Miranda to me were fairly unusual, the guardianship can be legalized—if I consent."

Laura nodded, her attention squarely on him. She was practically quivering in her chair. He knew damn well that she wanted to prod him for more information. But she wouldn't, so he took pity on her.

"And no, I haven't called child welfare."

She released a pent-up breath.

"But that's not saying I won't."

Her lips tightened.

Why should she be able to make him feel guilty?

He hardly knew her. Of course, she made him feel lots of *other* things, too. Don't go there, he told himself silently. "Laura, it's too early for me to decide anything."

"I understand," she said tightly.

"That's nice," he returned. "I'm not sure I do."

"What do you mean?"

He glanced at the baby. She was smearing her green beans across the tray of the high chair. Her soft, fine hair was dotted with leftover mashed potatoes, and a stream of drool was running down her chin.

Just looking at the small disaster area should have made up his mind for him. Why it didn't was beyond him.

Jeff shook his head wearily. "I don't understand why I can't decide what to do."

Over the next few days, the three of them settled into an uneasy routine. While Jeff was at the base, Laura concentrated on Miranda, trying to keep the captain out of her mind entirely. Sometimes, she would even go hours without once thinking about him.

But eventually, thoughts of him drifted across her brain, and she snatched at them like a child grabbing for the string of an escaped balloon.

Laura groaned, closed her mind to thoughts of Jeff and concentrated instead on bathing the baby. A task that seemed to be never ending.

Jeff took the stairs to the third floor of the old building and stopped as he entered the hall leading to his apartment. Mrs. Butler, just a step or two ahead of him, was staggering under the weight of an overstuffed grocery bag.

Instantly, he hurried to her side and lifted the bag from her painfully thin arms. "Didn't you tell me a couple of weeks ago you were going to start having the groceries delivered?"

She glared up at him out of the blue eyes that marked his every movement. "They charge extra for that, y'know," she told him, then scuttled to her apartment door, Jeff right behind her.

"Wouldn't it be worth it?" he asked. The older woman was as stubborn as she was nosy. Once, he'd even offered to get the old bat one of those rolling carts to carry her groceries in. She had informed him that only *old,* old people used those things and she wasn't that bad off yet.

When she had the last of her locks opened, she pushed the door open, then turned to him, reaching for the bag. "I'm keeping a close watch on you and that baby, mister," she said, her voice as creaky as an old iron gate.

"I never doubted it for a minute, Mrs. Butler."

"Humph!" She sniffed pointedly. "That woman you got staying with you seems nice enough."

A compliment? Stop the presses.

The woman's features softened considerably for a moment. "Saw the two of them today," she said. "Out for a walk, they were. That Miranda is a doll."

Jeff smiled to himself. Who would have guessed that his nemesis had a soft spot for babies?

She spotted that smile.

Her features stiffened. Snatching the bag of groceries, she stepped into her apartment and slammed the door shut.

Grinning now, Jeff listened for the four locks to be set in place before calling out, "You're welcome."

Leaning over the edge of the bathtub, Laura smiled down at the chubby little face turned up at her. Miranda's two small hands clutched a bright yellow rubber duck that squeaked if the little girl managed to squeeze it hard enough.

The baby, chattering happily in a language all her own, suddenly smashed the duck down into the water, splashing Laura's face and chest.

"Well, thank you," she said, swiping one hand across her eyes, then pushing wet hair off her forehead.

Miranda laughed, tipping her little head back and closing her eyes tightly with delight. Then, smacking her open palms against the surface of the water, she watched the duck rock in the resulting waves.

"Having fun?" A deep voice from right behind her startled Laura, and she gasped aloud.

"You scared me," she snapped, glaring at him over one shoulder.

"Sorry." He leaned against the doorjamb and looked down at the two of them. "Thought you heard me come in."

"Not likely," Laura told him, jerking her head toward the baby.

One corner of his mouth lifted. "She is a little loud, isn't she?" Then his gaze settled on the dampness on Laura's shirt and the slicked-back hair on top of her head. "Thought you were supposed to be bathing *her,* not the other way around."

God, he looked great, Laura thought before her good sense could prevent it. If the big-name clothing designers could just see him, they'd hustle out a spring line of camouflage wear. She inhaled slowly, deeply, and reminded herself that she no longer noticed how good-looking a man was. That was something she put behind her years ago.

Sure. So why was her pulse racing as though she'd just completed a marathon? Oh, she needed some distance between herself and the captain.

"As long as you're home early," she said, coming up on her knees, "you can finish bathing the baby while I fix something for dinner."

He straightened up and stiffened like he'd been shot. Against the dark greens and browns of his uniform, his face paled. His gaze shot from her to the baby and back again.

"No way," he declared, holding one hand up, palm out. "Uh-uh. The deal was *you* take care of the baby."

If she wasn't in such a hurry to get away from him, this whole thing might have been laughable. "I also said I wouldn't be the cook around here, either," she reminded him. "But *who* has been doing the lion's share of that lately?"

He frowned at her. "I didn't ask you to cook for me."

"That's not the point," she said, and spared a glance for Miranda. The little girl was still happily busy with her duck. "The point *is,* now that you're here, we can share some of the chores."

"Fine," he said, and half turned to leave. "I'll cook."

"Lord, no!" she snapped, remembering the salmon steak he had broiled two nights before. If the poor fish had been as tough when it was alive, it would have been able to pull the fisherman who caught it into the ocean and beat the heck out of him with its fins.

"Come on, *Marine*." She said it slowly, sarcastically, making sure he heard her mentally throwing down the gauntlet. "You can handle a *baby* for a few minutes, can't you?"

Hell, Jeff thought. He could hardly handle being in the same room with Laura! Her cheeks were flushed with the warm, moist air in the bathroom, tendrils of brown hair curled softly around her face and her eyes looked dewy, despite the spark of challenge she was shooting at him.

His insides twisted with an unexpected pang. Obviously, he thought in disgust, his attraction for her hadn't weakened any, despite his hopes.

Jeez, only a week ago, he was a perfectly content man. His life and career were running smoothly. Now, everything around him was in turmoil.

All because of one small person.

Jeff let his gaze slide from Laura's flushed cheeks to the little girl sitting in the tub. Bubbles drifted past the sturdy, chubby body, and as they did, Miranda tried to catch them with quick, clumsy movements. Something inside him shifted as he watched the child.

He'd done his best to keep a safe distance between him and the tiny interloper. But no matter where he went in his apartment, evidence of her presence was already there. Her bottles, blankets and toys were strewn across the once painfully neat place.

He no longer walked barefoot through his house anymore, since the night his arch slammed down on the straight edge of a pacifier. He didn't sleep late on his days off, and even staying up late was out of the question because he couldn't play his stereo at the deafening levels he preferred.

One small scrap of humanity had completely altered his life.

Hell, Mrs. Butler had smiled at him!

At that moment, Miranda looked up at him and gave him a wide, sloppy grin. Twin dimples deepened her fat cheeks. Blue eyes sparkled with life and laughter. An infectious, rolling giggle shot from her throat, and he found himself reluctantly returning that silly smile.

Something warm and soft and completely alien to him settled in his chest. He didn't want to like it. He tried to ignore it. Tried to pretend he didn't feel a thing when he looked at that baby.

But the bottom line was, she was reaching him as no other female ever had.

And that scared the hell out of him.

"Well?" Laura asked, drawing him back from his terrifying thoughts. "Are you going to take over or not?"

He could do this, he told himself. He was a captain in the United States Marine Corps. He could damn well bathe a six-month-old infant. In his career, he had survived enemy gunfire, eager new recruits and overbearing officers.

One little girl was *not* going to defeat him.

"Okay," he said, stepping into the small room. "I'll do it."

"Kneel down here," Laura told him, scooting over a bit.

He didn't particularly want to be that close to Laura at the moment, either. If Miranda tugged at his heart-strings, Laura touched him on a much deeper, more basic level. Yet she managed to scare him every bit as badly as the baby did.

"Wouldn't this be easier if you moved out of the way first?" he asked shortly.

She shot him a look usually reserved for a dog who'd made a mess on the carpet. "*Never* leave a baby alone in a bathtub."

"She's not alone," he protested even as he surrendered and kneeled down beside Laura. "I'm right here."

"Anything can happen," she told him, her features serious, her gaze lancing into his. "In a matter of seconds, an untended baby can drown in just a couple of inches of water."

"For God's sake," he said harshly, "I'm not going to toss her into a lake and tell her to swim for it."

Laura laid one hand on his. A wild electrical current seemed to spring into life between them. He felt a sharp, jagged blast of heat rocket up his arm and burst in his chest like a mortar shell.

He knew being close to her was a bad idea.

She must have felt it, too, because she pulled back instantly. When she spoke again, her voice shook a bit.

He didn't blame her. He felt a little shaky himself.

"I mean it, Jeff. Don't take your eyes off of her for an instant."

This is what he got for hesitating when she asked him to take over. Now Laura probably figured that he was too incompetent to wash a child.

"I think I can handle the responsibility," he assured her, the words dripping with a sarcasm she apparently didn't notice.

"I'll check on you in a minute."

"That's not necessary," he said as she stood up and moved around him.

"It's no trouble," she told him. "I'll just go throw the steaks on the broiler. If you need help—"

"When people need help," he interrupted, reaching down into the tub for the rubber duck, "they usually *send* for the Marines."

Unimpressed, she retorted, "Yeah? Well, then who do you guys call for help?"

Slanting her a long look over his shoulder, he said proudly, "There's only one force stronger than us."

She paused in the doorway, obviously curious. "Who's that?"

"There's the U.S. Marines...and then there's God."

Five

Halfway through the bath, Jeff was silently calling on that higher power in desperation.

"C'mon, Miranda," he said, and winced at the pleading note in his voice. "If you don't sit still, we can't get the job done."

She laughed at him and slithered out of his grasp like a greased piglet.

Jeff reached for her and tried his Marine voice. Stiff, stern, demanding attention. "All right, recruit. Straighten up."

She flipped onto her tummy and started crawling across the floor of the tub. Exasperated, Jeff lunged for her. After he had her, though, he turned her around to face him, and she slapped both of his cheeks with bubble-covered hands. He blew the soapy water off his lips and managed to close his eyes in time to avoid the tidal wave of water she kicked at him.

Bubbles cascaded down his face as the wet soaked into the front of his cammies. His knees slid on the bathroom rug, and his chest slammed into the edge of the tub. His grip on the baby didn't loosen, though. Grumbling under his breath, he plopped her down again and grabbed a neatly folded washcloth.

"You and I have to come to an understanding, kiddo," he said as he ran the soaped cloth over first one arm, then the other.

She kicked her legs in the water, splashing him again.

He sighed, resigned now to the cold, clinging material of his uniform. Reaching for one foot, he rubbed the cloth over her pink skin. "You've pretty much been calling the shots around here, you know?"

She giggled deep in her throat.

He reached for the other foot. "But if you're going to be staying here—" he heard that statement come out of his mouth and quickly amended it "—for *a while,* you've got to understand that *you're* the private and *I'm* the captain."

She giggled again and tried to pull her foot free. He held on.

"We do things *my* way in this outfit," he went on, rubbing the cloth over her arch again just so he could hear that giggle.

She didn't disappoint him. Then she leaned over, her little fingers tugging and pulling at his hands.

"Ticklish, huh?" he asked with a smile.

The baby scooted around on her bottom, flashing him another grin.

He dropped the washcloth into the soapy water and lifted her, his hands beneath her fat little arms.

She clapped her hands and kicked her feet, but he had taken the precaution of lifting her high enough that she couldn't soak him again.

"We did it," he said. "Got through the bath with no problems. See? All you have to do is remember who's in charge around here and we'll get along fine."

As if in answer, he heard the distinct sound of water trickling into water.

Looking at Miranda through wary eyes, he saw her self-satisfied smile and knew instantly what she'd done.

"Oh, man..." he said on a defeated sigh.

The town park was crowded on Saturdays.

Sunshine poured from a sky so blue it almost hurt to look at it. A few puffs of white clouds danced in the breeze that lifted kites high over the treetops.

Keeping a close eye on Miranda, Laura sat on the quilt Jeff had spread out on the grass beneath an ancient oak tree and watched the parade of people whirl by.

Bicyclists in helmets, pads and skintight suits raced along the path winding through the park, darting around slower-paced strollers pushed by proud fathers and tired-looking mothers. A few in-line skaters roared past her, their wheels grinding on the pavement with a soft whirr. Off to one side, two boys were playing catch with their father, and in the sand-filled playground to the left of her, smaller children were gathered. Toddlers laughed as they scrambled over concrete statues of dinosaurs and bounced on fiberglass ponies mounted on stiff springs.

Laura sighed and smiled. It had been a lovely afternoon, she thought lazily. She'd been surprised but touched when Jeff had suggested a picnic. Maybe he was getting used to the idea of having a baby in his life. She glanced at the little girl scooting across the blanket with determined, crablike movements.

Laura leaned forward, scooped her up and sat her down again, this time safely trapping the baby between her legs.

Over the past few days, Jeff hadn't again mentioned finding a replacement guardian for Miranda, and Laura was sure that was a good sign. Given enough time, the sweet baby would be able to worm her way into even an ogre's heart.

And Jeff Ryan was no ogre.

Despite what he seemed to think.

Miranda watched the children playing. Her little hands clapping, she made another stab at an escape, but was easily bought off with a teething biscuit.

Tired, Laura looked off toward the parking lot, where she could just see Jeff closing up the car again and starting back toward them, Miranda's sweater in his hand.

Honestly, she thought. The man looked good enough to be illegal. Even from a distance, she could see how well his faded, threadbare Levi's fit his long legs. And the red polo shirt he wore made his blond hair seem lighter, while at the same time giving his tan a deeper, warmer tone.

And here she sat, huddled under a tree, because the slightest amount of sunshine made her look like a boiled lobster.

Her heartbeat stuttered into high gear. Silently groaning, Laura tried to ignore what had become an all too familiar sensation lately. Two weeks, she thought. Two weeks with Jeff and Miranda and she was a goner. Oh, she'd been prepared to fall in love with the baby. She never had been able to resist one. But Jeff was another matter entirely.

She'd sworn off love a long time ago. And in all the years since, she had never once been tempted to fall off the wagon.

Until now.

As he came closer, Laura studied him, trying to ignore her quickened heartbeat and the rush of adrenaline. What was it about him that created such a wild tangle of emotions?

He smiled, and lifted one hand in greeting just as a boy on a skateboard sped past him. Laura laughed shortly as Jeff did a fancy two-step to avoid falling. The expression on his face was priceless.

Shaking his head, he stepped off the path onto the grass and headed straight for her.

It was as if a steel band had tightened around her chest. Lord help her. If she hadn't already given up on love, Jeff Ryan would definitely be a man to watch out for.

Jeff studied her as he approached. In a park full of women wearing shorts and clingy T-shirts, why was he so completely taken with a woman dressed in baggy jeans and a T-shirt that would have been big on him? Her hair was pulled back into a ponytail at the base of her neck, and a few wisps of shorter hair flew about her cheeks.

Their gazes locked, and as she tucked a strand of hair behind her ear, he noticed that she suddenly looked kind of sick. He sat down beside her in the shade, tossed Miranda's sweater to one side and asked, "You all right?"

"Yeah," she replied a little too quickly. "Why wouldn't I be?"

"You just looked a little..."

"What?" she asked.

"Nothing," he said, backing down. He wasn't in the mood for a fight now, and it sounded like she was. Whenever Laura's voice got that tight, controlled sound to it, he knew there was an argument headed his way. And it was just too nice a day for it. Who would have thought that he could enjoy a simple picnic so much? "Boy," he commented absently, "this place gets nuts on the weekend."

"It's the first nice day all week," she said.

He shot her a quick look, then turned away again, frowning. Were they really going to talk about the weather? There was so much he wanted to know about her. Like why a kindergarten teacher? Why wasn't she married? And if she loved kids so much, why didn't she have one or two of her own?

But mostly, did she want him as much as he wanted her?

He didn't ask any of his questions, though. For

some reason, he couldn't think of a way to start. Hell, he'd never had a hard time holding a conversation with a woman before. What was it about her that unsettled him so?

Miranda pulled herself across Laura's legs and crawled to him. Grateful for the distraction, Jeff lowered his gaze to the determined baby. Holding on to his shirtsleeve, she slowly drew herself up to wobble unsteadily on her bare feet. Her tiny toes curled into the blanket as if she were trying to get a grip on the world.

"Hey," he said, afraid to move lest he spoil her balance. "Look at you!" An unreasonable swell of pride filled his chest. She looked so pleased with herself, he suddenly wished he had a camera. Good Lord, what was happening to him? Then Miranda gurgled at him, and something around his heart tightened a notch.

"What a big girl you are!" he said.

Miranda laughed up at him and swayed as she patted his chest with one hand.

Chuckling, Jeff scooped her up in one arm and held her in front of him. The now familiar weight of her in his arms was comforting. She smelled of baby powder and giggles. It was a scent he would always remember.

With his thumb, he wiped away a streak of drool from her chin, realizing ruefully that only two weeks ago, he would have grabbed a paper towel to handle the small task. "You're something, kiddo," he said with a smile. "Don't you know you're too young to walk?" He glanced at Laura, suddenly unsure. Heck, he didn't have a clue what babies should be doing at any given age. "She *is*, isn't she?"

"Yes," she confirmed, with a slight shake of her head. "But not too young to be trying."

"Ooo-rah, Miranda," he said, looking back into blue eyes surprisingly like his own. "Always reach high, kiddo."

"Look out!" someone called a moment before a bright-blue-and-yellow ball bounced into the middle of the quilt.

Laura grabbed it just as a harried-looking mother ran up to them, apologies spilling from her lips. She looked like a magazine ad for the typical southern California mom. Short blond hair, healthy tan and a well-toned body displayed by white shorts and a pale yellow tank top.

"Sorry about that," she said, and took the ball Laura offered her. "My five-year-old's got quite a kick. His father is already planning his career in the NFL." She took a deep breath, tucked the ball beneath her right arm and bent down to take a good look at Miranda. Reaching out one hand, she chucked the baby's chin and sighed, "What a cute little girl."

"Yeah, she is," Jeff said shortly, not sure how to react to the woman. He shot Laura a quick glance and noted her proud smile as the stranger admired Miranda.

"She has your eyes," the woman commented, looking at him.

He frowned slightly, the sense of pride he'd experienced only moments before suddenly at war with a different emotion blossoming in his chest. An emotion that caused him to blurt out, "She's not mine."

The woman blinked.

Miranda bounced in his arms.

A brief, strained silence reigned before the woman then looked to Laura. "Sorry, my mistake. Your daughter's a beauty, though. Always wanted a girl myself." She shrugged and kept talking, as if to smooth over the tension in the air. "Instead, I got four boys." Turning a wistful look on Miranda, she muttered, "If somebody could guarantee me one like that, I'd be willing to go again."

"Hey, Mom!" a boy's voice hollered.

"Coming," the woman called back, and stood up. "Better get going," she said. "Sorry again." Then she turned and ran back toward her family.

Jeff watched her go with pleasure. If she hadn't interrupted a perfectly nice afternoon, he wouldn't now be feeling so...what? Guilty?

"Why'd you tell her Miranda wasn't yours?" Laura asked when they were alone again.

"Because she's not." Even to him, his voice sounded strangled, harsh.

"Maybe not biologically," she corrected. "But legally..."

Jeff's features tightened, and Laura couldn't help wondering what he was thinking. How could he hold that baby, play with her and take such obvious pride in the little things she did and still not want to claim her?

"You know," he said through clenched teeth, "it's real easy for you to say, 'She's yours—keep her.' But I don't see *you* with any kids. Why is that if you're so nuts about children?"

Laura paled. She felt the blood drain from her

cheeks and was helpless to stop it. "I'm not married," she hedged.

"Neither am I, in case you haven't noticed."

"This isn't about me," Laura countered, knowing it was a weak argument.

"Why not?" Jeff turned the baby around, plopped her down onto his lap and looked at Laura steadily. "Why don't we make this about you for a change?"

"I'd rather not talk about it."

"You don't have any trouble telling me what I should do with *my* life."

"Jeff..." Horrified, Laura felt the sting of tears fill her eyes. She dipped her head and hurriedly blinked them back.

"Come on, Laura," he prodded, "tell me. Why is someone who is so crazy about kids still single?"

When she thought she could trust herself not to cry, she lifted her head and looked at him. Apparently, her eyes were still awash with tears, though. The expression on his face was too stricken to mean anything else. Before he could speak, she sucked in a deep breath and said simply, "I was engaged once. He died."

"Oh, man..." Jeff sighed heavily, reached across the blanket and took one of her hands in his. Giving her a gentle squeeze, he said softly, "I'm sorry. I shouldn't have said anything."

"No," she told him. "You were right. It *is* easy for me to tell you to raise a child you hadn't counted on having." Her gaze dropped to Miranda, now happily gumming Jeff's thumb. "But I just don't understand how you could *not* want her."

"Wanting something...or *someone*, is one thing. Figuring out if it's the best thing for everyone is something else."

Seconds rolled into minutes, and the silence between them stretched on and on. Finally, Jeff asked quietly, "Do you still love him?"

She inhaled sharply. A few weeks ago, her answer would have been a quick, decisive yes. Now, if she was to be honest with herself, it was a different story. Lord, what was happening to her? "He'll always have a place in my heart," she said at last.

Jeff nodded slowly. "That doesn't answer the question."

She met his gaze. "It's the only answer I have."

The muscle in his jaw ticked spasmodically as he gave her a short, sharp nod.

"Here," he said abruptly, handing the baby over. "You take her while I go pack up the car."

"We're leaving?" she asked, cuddling the squirming baby close. "Already?"

"Yeah," he told her, gathering up the picnic basket and a couple of stray napkins. "I've got some things I should be doing back at the base."

"What things?" She had the distinct impression he was trying to run away. From her? To where? "I thought you had the day off."

"Just things, all right?" he snapped, and stood up quickly. He looked at her for a long minute, then said, "Get the baby ready—I'll be back."

He marched down the path, like a soldier going off to war. Eyes straight ahead, he looked neither right nor left, ignoring everyone and everything around him.

What had just happened here? she wondered. Did it bother him that much to know she would always care for Bill?

"And why is he fighting you so hard?" Laura asked the baby. "Why can't he just admit that he loves you? Is it really so hard for him?"

The baby blew a spit-bubble raspberry.

One eyebrow arched high on Laura's forehead. "My sentiments exactly."

That night, Jeff turned the stereo on, needing the soothing sounds of his favorite music. In deference to the baby, he kept the volume at a level just below earsplitting.

He had hardly plopped down onto the couch before Laura came out of her bedroom. That stupid nightshirt of hers looked ridiculously sexy, which told Jeff that he'd been without a woman way too long. After glaring at him for a minute, she strode to the stereo and pushed the Power button.

Silence dropped over the room like a heavy blanket.

"What are you doing?" she demanded, pushing her hair back behind her ears.

"Listening to music," he said, getting up from the couch. "Like I used to, every damn night."

He walked to the stereo and hit the Power switch with a stab of his index finger. Instantly, guitars roared into life.

Laura punched the same button a breath later. She stood, arms crossed, chin lifted, foot tapping solidly against the floor.

In the charged silence, Jeff stared down at her, anger

and frustration pulsing through him. He'd spent the entire night in his office on base, trying to keep busy enough that he didn't think about this frumpy, short woman who had invaded his life so thoroughly.

It hadn't worked.

Even now, when he wanted to scream and shout and rage at her, one question kept sliding through his mind. What color underwear was she wearing tonight?

Groaning, he reached up and shoved both hands along the sides of his head, as if he could quiet the fantasies that had nagged him all night.

Damn it, if she and the baby weren't there, everything would be fine. He wouldn't be dreaming about ugly nightgowns and gorgeous lingerie. He wouldn't be taking cold showers every morning and tiptoeing through the house at night.

Mrs. Butler wouldn't be smiling at him every time he passed her in the hall.

He could have his life back. The simple, uncomplicated life that he had never truly appreciated as much as he did now that he'd lost it.

But that wasn't going to happen, and he knew it. Even if Laura and Miranda were to disappear tonight, nothing would be the same as it had been before they'd come. Because no matter what, there were memories of the two of them. Vivid mental images that would always be with him.

He would never have true solitude again.

Gritting his teeth at the thought, he turned the music back on and grabbed Laura's hand before she could hit the button.

"Leave it on," he growled, his fingers tight around her small wrist.

"It'll wake the baby."

"She'll go back to sleep."

"When I first came here, I told you my rules," she said, jerking her hand from his grasp, then rubbing at the skin on her wrist.

"Your rules," he repeated with a short bark of laughter.

"That's right," she said. "And you agreed to them."

"I was desperate," he argued, unwillingly remembering that first, hideous day when he'd begged his sister for help, not knowing that he was asking for even more trouble than he already had.

"You still agreed."

"I would have agreed to a human sacrifice that day, and you damn well know it." He looked away from her, his throat aching with the effort of forcing angry words past a tight knot of anxiety.

"Why are you so upset?"

His gaze swung back to her instantly.

She reached for the stereo again, but instead of turning it off, she only lowered the volume.

The familiar beat of an old rock song thrummed in the darkness like a heartbeat. Seconds ticked by. At last, Jeff crossed the room to the wide window and opened the blinds.

"What is it?" she asked, pitching her voice just loud enough to be heard over a rattle of drums.

He felt more than heard her walk up behind him. It was as if he could sense her position in the room. Tiny electrical currents seemed to stretch from her to him, digging at him, prodding at him.

"Jeff?" she asked, closer now.

He inhaled sharply and shook his head, staring out at the neon patchwork quilt beyond the glass. "This isn't going to work," he finally said.

She stopped beside him. Heat from her body reached out to him, sinking into his bones. His soul. He sensed her gaze on his face and deliberately kept from looking at her.

"What's not going to work?" she asked, obviously not going to be put off.

A snort of laughter shot from his chest, and a hard knot of pain settled in its place.

"None of it's working, Laura. Not the baby…" He paused and glanced briefly at her. "Not you."

"You don't know it won't work. It's only been a couple of weeks."

God, just barely two weeks, and the world as he had known it was completely gone.

"Exactly," he said. He heard the snarl in his voice but was helpless to stop it.

"That's no time at all," she argued, tugging at his upper arm, trying to turn him toward her. "You haven't tried—"

With a low growl of frustration, Jeff turned on her. Grabbing her shoulders, he gave her a shake. There was no way out. He had to admit to the one shameful truth that he had realized only that night.

"Don't you get it?" he demanded, his voice slicing the music-filled air. "Maybe I don't *want* to try."

She yanked herself free. Anger flashed in her eyes,

and he was almost relieved. It was easier to deal with anger than disgust.

"So *this* is how you meet responsibility? You run from it? Find someone—*anyone* else to raise Miranda?"

"I'm not talking about letting her be raised by wolves, for Christ's sake."

"Why *not* wolves? As long as it's not you, what do you care who does it?"

"I want what's best for her," he said. "She deserves a family. People who know how to take care of kids. What to do for them." He shook his head. "You know as well as I do that's not me."

She planted her palms on his chest and shoved him with all of her strength.

He didn't budge.

Reaching up, Jeff rubbed the back of his neck viciously. "I'm thirty-five years old, Laura. I'm too old to learn this stuff." He inhaled sharply and blew it out on a heavy sigh. "I'm too old to become an overnight father."

Once the words were out, he felt as though he'd finally managed to shove a gigantic boulder off his chest. Maybe she would understand now, he told himself.

He should've known better.

"That's just an excuse," she snapped. "You're looking for an easy way out."

"Shouldn't I be?" he asked, leveling a long look on her. A wave of guilt and shame swamped him as he reached back to the moment earlier that afternoon that had slapped him with a harsh, undeniable reality.

One that even now he was having a hard time facing.

"Sergeant Powell trusted you," she said hotly. "He left you his *child*. That has to mean something to you."

"Why?" he growled. "Because it would to you?"

Laura's head snapped back as if he had slapped her.

Damn it. None of this was her fault. She didn't deserve to be yelled at just because she was handy. He tilted his head back on his neck and stared briefly at the shadowy ceiling. He concentrated on pulling what was left of his self-control together. But it wasn't easy.

Man, this was one of those times when he really wished he were a drinking man. But that was stupid. Even if he did go off and get roaring drunk, the situation he faced wouldn't have changed by the time he sobered up.

Jeff felt her staring at him and sensed the hurt in her. He was really batting a thousand. He couldn't seem to make the call to child welfare that would get him out of this mess. And hurting the woman who was there to help him.

Shifting to look at Laura again, he tried to explain what he meant.

"Look," he said tightly, "I never *wanted* kids. It's not that I don't like 'em," he added. "I like my sister's kids fine."

"It's a wonder you don't go and visit more than once a year, then," she countered stiffly.

Thanks, Peggy, he thought. He sucked in a gulp of air, trying to ease the knot of helpless anger practically choking him. "Damn it, Laura, I decided a long time ago that I wasn't going to *have* a family. I wanted a career and I figured rather than do two things halfway, I'd do one thing well.''

Her brown eyes shone with a film of tears that he hoped to God she wouldn't let spill over.

In a quieter tone, he added, ''Not everybody in the world *wants* kids, you know.''

Her head bobbed in an abbreviated nod.

''I have my own plans. Plans that don't include kids.'' He looked away from her, out at the night. His hands curling around the windowsill, he continued, ''I didn't know Hank had named me as guardian to Miranda.'' Quietly, he added, ''If I had, I would have told him not to.''

''Everybody makes plans, Jeff,'' she said, her voice as soft as his had been.

''You, too?'' He asked, then remembered the late fiancé.

''Of course, me too.''

''You *planned* to be a temporary nanny?'' He didn't want to talk about the man she had once loved— maybe still *did* love.

She chuckled and he felt a bit better.

''No,'' she answered.

''What happened?'' he asked, half turning to look at her. Damn. He didn't want to know and yet he did. *Nothing* made sense anymore.

''The same thing that happened to you.'' She shrugged eloquently. ''Life. And when life shakes up your plans, you have to adapt. To accept.''

He stared at her thoughtfully. She may have accepted, but she hadn't adapted.

"It's not easy," she said, her voice dropping a bit. "But you do it anyway."

"I don't know," he answered, his grip on the windowsill relaxing a bit. "All I *do* know is, in the park, when that woman said Miranda looked like me—" he shook his head and forced himself to say it all "—my first instinct was to deny all claim to her. I knew that if I claimed her in that moment, then it was decided forever. There'd be no going back. I wasn't ready to make that decision." He pulled in another deep breath and exhaled on a rush. "What kind of father is that?"

The remainder of Laura's anger drained away instantly. She heard pain and confusion in his tone. She knew he was ashamed of his reaction to that woman's innocent statement and that he was trying to deal with it.

"It was completely natural," she said softly.

He laughed shortly and shot her a sidelong look. "Natural to say, 'No, no, that's not *my* baby.'"

"You're not used to her yet."

When he spoke, his words came so softly, Laura had to lean in close to hear him.

"What if I *never* get used to her?"

Six

Laura took a long, deep breath and laid her hand on his forearm. An instantaneous burst of heat rocketed up her own arm, settling in her chest. She tried to dismiss the sensation and concentrate.

The muscles beneath her hand flinched at her touch.

"Is it fair to Miranda," he asked through gritted teeth, "to be raised by a man who might *never* be the kind of father she deserves?"

Laura felt a rush of warmth that had nothing to do with the chemistry between them well up inside her. She had thought he didn't care. That he didn't want to be bothered by the responsibility of Miranda.

She'd been wrong.

"I'm sorry," she said suddenly, and he swiveled her a look.

"About what?"

This wasn't easy, she thought, but it had to be said.

"I thought you didn't care about the baby, but I should have known better." She shook her head slightly. "I've watched you with her. You *do* feel something for her."

"She's not easy to ignore," he said, a rueful smile on his face.

"True." Laura steeled herself. "But mostly, I'm sorry for what I was thinking about you."

Two blond eyebrows lifted. "An intriguing statement."

Now it was her turn to give him a reluctant smile. "You were right. I did expect you to want the baby because *I* would have in your shoes." Shaking her head slightly, she said, "It's just that I always wanted kids of my own. I guess I was judging you by my feelings. Arrogant, I know." Throwing both hands up in a helpless shrug, she continued. "You have every right to *not* want kids. Not everyone does. Besides, I know what a huge responsibility she would be for a man like you."

"Like me?"

"Single, career oriented."

"Ah…"

She wasn't quite sure how to interpret that last comment, so she left it alone. "All I'm saying is that I'm sorry. I, better than anyone, should have remembered what it's like to have your life's plan splintered in one quick blow."

She hadn't meant to give him that much information. It would have been too much to hope for that he would ignore it.

"What happened to your neatly arranged world, Laura?" he asked, his voice dropping to mingle with the deep, fluid notes of the music swelling around them. "What little bombshell did Fate drop on you?"

"It doesn't matter," she said. Laura didn't want to explain about Bill. For some reason, she felt as though this moment, this night, belonged only to her and Jeff. Not even memories were welcome. "This is about you, not me."

His features tight, worry lines deepened at the corners of his eyes and between his eyebrows. His mouth a grim slash, she knew he wanted to ask her more questions. But Laura was through talking about herself. Determinedly, she went back to their original subject, hoping he would leave her past where it belonged.

"You would be a good father," she said firmly.

He frowned, clearly not happy with the shift in the conversation. But he went along with it. "Yeah? What makes you so sure?"

"Because you're already worried about doing the job right. A bad father wouldn't care either way."

He seemed to think about that for a long minute. Then slowly, the muscle in his arm relaxed. Reluctantly, she let her hand drop to her side.

"Maybe," he finally said, his gaze caressing her face. "I don't know."

"You'll see." She wanted him to believe her.

He lifted one hand and smoothed her hair back from her face. The pad of his thumb stroked her cheekbone, sending a trembling response through her body.

"Don't misunderstand me," he told her, his voice

as soft as his touch. "I'm not saying anything's changed. I'm still not convinced that Miranda being with me is the right thing for her. Or me."

Laura stared at him, confused. Hadn't they just been discussing that very thing? "But I thought—"

"I know," he said, and let his fingertips trail along the length of her throat. "And I appreciate what you said. But this is a big decision, Laura. One I'm not going to make overnight."

It wasn't fair of him to touch her while talking to her about something this serious. She couldn't concentrate. All she could do was feel. It had been so long, she thought, her eyes sliding shut. So long since anyone had touched her like this. So long since she had *wanted* a man's touch.

But it wasn't just any man she wanted, she admitted silently.

It was *this* man.

She moaned softly at the realization.

For eight long years, she had kept her heart, her emotions carefully locked away. After Bill's death, she had buried her wants and desires. She'd thrown herself into her work, satisfied with teaching and loving other people's children.

Now, suddenly, it wasn't enough.

Maybe it never had been.

Jeff stepped in closer to her, as if sensing her surrender.

His hands moved to her shoulders, and she felt the warmth of his touch right down to her soul. The dark corners of her heart were filled with a searing light that banished shadows and illuminated desires.

Moonlight poured through the window, bathing them both in a pale ivory glow. A new song drifted from the stereo. The rock guitars had given way to a slow jazz piano and a soulful saxophone. The plaintive notes of the horn sounded like stereo sex.

Hot, slow and mesmerizing.

She swallowed heavily.

His right hand dropped to her waist. "Dance with me," he whispered.

Laura knew she should say no. As vulnerable as she felt at the moment, the safest place for her to be was somewhere far away from him. But she couldn't refuse. Already, her body was surrendering to the seductive music.

Sliding her left hand up onto his shoulder, she stepped into his embrace. Her right hand caught by his left, she felt the surprisingly erotic sensation of their palms brushing together.

He began moving in a slow, tight circle. He swayed slightly with the rhythm of the music, and she moved with him. His arm around her waist tightened, pulling her closer to him. Her breasts flattened against his chest, she felt his heartbeat thundering in time with her own.

Her knees weak, Laura's breath caught when his denim-clad thighs rubbed her bare legs. His right hand slipped to cup her bottom, pressing her tight enough to him that she was aware of his own need and knew it was as powerful as the sexual flames licking at her center.

The sensuous music rose up and around them, drawing the two of them together, into a net built of the breathless desire shimmering between them. Shadows and moonlight shifted around her as she stared up into his eyes. Her breathing shallow, her heartbeat quickened even further until her pulse became nothing more than a thundering roar in her ears.

She knew the moment he decided to kiss her. She read it on his face and realized that this was her last chance to escape. In the same instant, she admitted silently that she didn't want to run. For the first time in eight long years, she wanted to feel.

If only for one night.

Then he bent his head to hers, and all thought stopped. His mouth dusted across her lips gently, tentatively. Drawing his head back, he looked down at her, his features tight with an emotion she didn't want to explore too closely.

One dance ended and another began.

He stopped, and moved his hands to cup her face. Then he kissed her again, and from behind closed eyes, Laura saw the bright flash of exploding stars.

He parted her lips with his tongue, his breath invading her mouth even as his kiss conquered her soul. Laura groaned quietly and leaned into him. A film of tears burned her eyes as a sweet ache began to grow within her.

He grabbed her and pulled her hard against him. Laura's arms wound around his neck, and she pressed herself as tightly to him as she could. Her hardened nipples throbbed for his touch. Her knees weak, she sagged into him as his tongue continued to plunder the defenses she had maintained for too long.

Jeff broke the kiss and bent his head lower, dragging his mouth along the line of her throat, tasting her pulse beat beneath his teeth. When she sighed and tipped her head to one side, allowing him access, he muffled a groan against her neck. His body aching, he inhaled her scent and knew he would carry it with him always.

The magic in her kiss was like nothing he had ever known.

Her skin was as soft as he had imagined it would be. Her fingers tugged and pulled at his shoulders, holding him tightly, silently urging him on.

Lifting the hem of her nightshirt, his right hand dropped to explore the curve of the bottom he had dreamed about so often. When his palm encountered only smooth, warm flesh, his breath was trapped in his lungs.

Straightening slightly, he looked down at her, an amazed half smile on his lips. "Here I've been trying to imagine what kind of lacy delight you were wearing under this hideous shirt—" he shook his head, stunned "—and you're not wearing any underwear at all."

She looked insulted. "Of course I'm wearing underwear."

"But..." He ran one hand over the bare flesh of her behind. It was only then that he noticed the tiny thread of fabric lining the cleft of her bottom. His fingertips smoothed across it, following it down. Shaken, he whispered, "A thong?"

She shivered as his fingers explored her, but finally, she nodded.

"Good God," he murmured huskily, his mind providing the image it was too dark to see. His groin hardened until he thought he might explode. "What color?"

She rose up on tiptoe to whisper in his ear. "Red."

"You're killing me, Laura." He groaned then and reclaimed her mouth, his tongue dipping in and out of her warmth in a hunger that built with each passing moment.

Scooping her up into his arms, he carried her to the sofa and sat down with her on his lap. Kissing, tasting, nibbling at her bottom lip with his teeth, Jeff reveled in her, exploring her body as thoroughly as he had dreamed of doing for days.

Sliding his hand up under the hem of her nightshirt, his fingertips encountered the scrap of red lace that was his undoing. He didn't need to see her. All he needed at the moment was to touch her.

She arched into his arms, her legs parting slightly for him. Devouring her mouth with his, he slid his right hand beneath that bit of lace and down to the damp heat that was at her core. Laura trembled in his arms as his hand cupped her.

Stirred by her response, Jeff drew his head back to look at her. He stared down into her face while slipping his fingertips farther, deeper into the secrets she guarded with lace barriers.

"Jeff," she whispered brokenly, and licked her lips with the tip of her tongue.

Something inside him shifted, but he swallowed back the groan of hunger roaring through him.

She lifted her hips when he dipped first one finger and then two deep within her. His breathing short and shallow, he indulged himself in her. In counterpoint to the raging desire coursing through his bloodstream, he explored her slowly, lazily. Her heat burned him; her passion fed his own. He bit back another groan as he watched pleasure steal across her features.

Again and again, his fingers moved within her, forcing her higher, faster as she strained to reach the completion awaiting her. Dipping his head, he kissed her, needing to taste her mouth and feel the intimate connection of their tongues mating.

Her response was instantaneous. Her tongue twisted and brushed around his in a silent erotic dance. She gave and took, submitted and conquered.

Gently but firmly, his thumb stroked across the small, sensitive nub of flesh. Her body jerked in his arms. She broke the kiss, moaning his name in a tearing whisper.

Her fingers clutched at his shoulders. Her body writhed in his arms, and when the first violent tremors shook her, Jeff felt the force of them himself. Tears leaked from the corners of her eyes as her hips rocked frantically against his hand. He claimed her mouth again in desperation, swallowing the last of her cries and using them to muffle his own.

Laura lay across his lap, feeling practically boneless. Relief shimmered through her even as inside her body, tiny, rippling convulsions still trembled on. She'd never experienced anything like that before. Had her climax been so overwhelming simply because it had been so long since her last one?

No, she decided, not without a pang of guilt. It was more than that. As much as she had loved Bill, he had never taken her so high…made her feel so much.

Instantly, that small sliver of guilt blossomed and grew. What was she thinking? How could she possibly compare what she had had with her fiancé to what she had just experienced? She had *loved* Bill. Hadn't she?

Of course she had. If he hadn't died, they would have been married eight years now. She would no doubt be the mother she had always longed to be. And she would be having regular, loving sex with her husband.

No doubt, with practice, she assured herself, their lovemaking would have become every bit as stimulating as—she bit down hard on her bottom lip—as stimulating as this first time with Jeff had been.

Oh, goodness, she thought, a sinking sensation developing in the pit of her stomach. If his hands alone could drive her above and beyond anything she had ever reached before, what might his actual lovemaking do to her?

Slowly, she tried to straighten up on Jeff's lap. Tugging at the hem of her nightshirt, she scooted her hips back and instantly gasped as a new rush of sensation poured through her. His hand was still cupping her, his fingers still deeply rooted within her passage.

"Laura," he whispered, his breath brushing against her cheek. "That was—"

"Please don't say anything," she interrupted him.

"I have to," he continued, and dropped a quick, firm kiss on the corner of her mouth.

Deep inside her, Laura felt the strength of his fingers, pressing against the walls of her body. Unbelievably, her muscles contracted around his hand, drawing him in, welcoming his touch. It was as if she had no defenses against him.

"Jeff," she managed to say, and grabbed his hand, hoping to stop him. "This was a mistake," she said, and knew it for the understatement of the century.

He lifted his head and smiled gently at her. "The only mistake we made was waiting so long to try it."

"No," she said even as his thumb brushed across that one incredibly sensitive spot again. "Oh!" Her breath caught as her body exploded into need again. No, it couldn't be. Not so soon. Not after what she had already experienced.

"Laura," he said, claiming short, damp kisses to punctuate each word, "this is special. This is right."

"No." She had to argue. This couldn't be right. If it was right, then what had she felt for Bill all those years ago?

"Yes," he insisted, moving within her, touching, stroking.

Her hips ground against his hand. Beneath her bottom, she felt the solid, thick ridge of his need pressing into her. He had given her release. He had taken her to heights she hadn't known existed, all the while ignoring his own clamoring desire.

The night pressed down on them. Music, low and full, surrounded them. Laura, knowing that she would regret this later, reached for the button at his waistband.

He sat perfectly still, his gaze locked with hers. "You don't have to, Laura."

But she did. Tomorrow would be soon enough to deal with *should have*s and *would have*s. Tonight, she wanted to feel everything she had denied herself for eight long, lonely years.

Leaning into him, she covered his mouth with her own, teasing him with long strokes of her tongue even as her fingers quickly undid the button fly of his jeans.

He sighed into her mouth as she took him in her hand. Her fingers caressed the hard length of him and gently rubbed the tip of his erection. His body tensed beneath her. His fingers dipped in and out of the liquid heat at her center.

When he finally groaned, pulled his hand free of her and in one quick move, yanked her red thong off and threw it onto the floor, she was beyond ready. His hands at her waist, he turned her on his lap until she was straddling him, their faces only a breath apart.

Kneeling on the sofa, her hands on his shoulders, Laura slowly lowered her body onto his. Inch by slow inch, she took him inside. His hands at her waist tightened, his fingers digging into her flesh. She sighed and moved on him again, rocking her hips slightly until she had welcomed him fully into her depths.

Laura's head tipped back. Her eyes closed, she concentrated on the incredible feel of him locked deeply within her. She twisted her hips in a slow, torturous pattern, moaning softly at the overwhelming sensations sputtering through her.

Jeff whispered her name and slid his hands up under her nightshirt, then pulled it off over her head. He tossed it to one side and captured her breasts with his palms. His thumbs rubbed at her hardened nipples until her breathing staggered.

As he tugged and pulled gently at the rigid peaks,

Laura moved on him. Her hips lifted and lowered as expectation built low in her belly. She knew it was coming. Knew how overpowering it would be. And she raced toward it, eager to feel it again. To ride the crashing waves of satisfaction as they thundered through her.

Jeff watched her. Moonlight dusted across her flesh, dazzling her in a pale glow that made her seem like part of a dream. But if this was a dream, he never wanted to wake up.

Reluctantly, he dropped his hands from her magnificent, full breasts. Grabbing her hips, he guided her into a quicker rhythm. Each time she took him inside, it felt like the first time. Each time she lifted herself from him, he died a little.

She raised her head and looked at him. He saw the swirl of passion dancing in her eyes. Her features tightened. Her back arched. Her lips parted, and she cried his name aloud as a shuddering climax claimed her.

Her interior muscles contracted around his body. He groaned and held her down on him tightly as he exploded into her warmth.

When it was over, Laura sagged against his chest. She felt his arms go around her and was numbly grateful for the support.

Every muscle in her body was almost liquid. Yet at the same time, she felt more *alive* than ever before. Her head on his shoulder, Laura listened to the ragged gasps of his breathing and knew that she wasn't the only one so completely affected by their lovemaking.

Lovemaking.

No, she couldn't think of it like that. This was sex. Pure, simple, glorious sex. Lovemaking had been what she had done with Bill, the man who would have been her husband.

The passion she shared with the man beneath her had nothing to do with love. It was something much more basic, more elemental than that. Lust, she supposed, was an old-fashioned word. But it certainly seemed to fit the situation.

Suddenly uncomfortable, Laura eased herself off of Jeff and groped in the darkness for her discarded nightshirt. When she found it, she immediately pulled it on.

"Laura," Jeff said softly. "I think we should talk about this."

She was profoundly thankful for the shadows filling the room. At the moment, she didn't want to be able to see his face too clearly. Shoving her hair back from her face, Laura glanced at him, then averted her gaze again, instead looking in the grayness for the thong panties she'd been wearing.

"I don't think that's necessary," she said. Spotting the tiny triangle of lace and elastic draped over the arm of a chair, Laura got up from the sofa to retrieve it.

Her knees were weak, and her body ached in places that hadn't been used in years. She stumbled a bit, caught herself and went on. Snatching up the red lace, she crumpled the pair of panties in one fist.

Her underwear, tossed across the room by a man caught up in the throes of passion. Good Lord, what had they been thinking? What had *she* been thinking?

He stood up and came around the coffee table to stand in front of her. He had already adjusted his clothing. To look at him, no one would guess what had just happened between them.

She envied him that control.

"I didn't mean for this to happen," he said, reaching for her.

Laura took a quick sidestep away from him. "Neither of us did, Jeff," she told him, and hoped her voice sounded steadier to him than it did to her. "But we're both adults. I'm sure we can put this behind us."

"Behind us?" he asked.

The lacy garment in her hand scratched against her palm. Laura knew she would never again be able to wear the panties without remembering this night and the stolen passion that had ignited something inside her. Something she hadn't even known existed.

Swallowing heavily, she said, "Jeff, I know you're trying to be...nice about all of this, but I really would rather not talk about it now." Or ever, she added silently.

He lifted one hand toward her, but let it fall to his side before touching her.

"Laura..." he started to say.

Thankfully, Miranda chose just that moment to cry. More of a whimper than a wail, at the moment it sounded like the sweetest music in the world to Laura. The baby crying provided just the excuse she needed to make a graceful escape.

She made it as far as the bedroom door before his voice stopped her. Closing her eyes and holding her breath, she prayed that he would let her go.

"Not tonight," he said, a promise ringing in his tone. "But we will talk about what happened, Laura. I'm too old to play games about something like this." He paused a moment. "And so are you."

She didn't answer. She couldn't have spoken if her life had depended on it. Turning the knob, she opened the door, slipped into the dark room and closed the door firmly behind her.

Briefly, she leaned back against that door, thinking about the man on the other side. How had this all become so confusing? she asked herself.

And how would she ever survive the entire summer here?

Seven

Jeff stretched out on his bed and turned his head on the pillow to stare at the doorway of his room. He heard her moving around in her room and the soft sound of her voice as she soothed Miranda back into sleep.

He groaned and punched a closed fist against the mattress. What kind of a twisted man was he that listening to a woman crooning to an infant could make him hard and eager for her?

It took every ounce of willpower he possessed to lie where he was and not go to Laura. He wanted an explanation. He wanted to know why there had been such incredible heat between them. And he wanted to feel it all again.

Basically, he thought grimly, he wanted her.

Again and again.

Inhaling sharply, he jammed his pillows behind his head, laid one arm across his chest and shifted his gaze to the ceiling.

Damn it. He didn't need this complication. Especially now. He hadn't expected to be drawn to such a frumpy little thing. Jeff snorted at the thought. Frumpy? He remembered his first sight of that red lace thong, the thin bands of elastic stretched across her small curves.

Beneath the hideous clothes she insisted on wearing was a body that could drive a man insane.

No, she wasn't frumpy. But she was warm and kind and gentle. All the things he'd tried to steer clear of in a woman for years.

Damn it, he should be feeling better. He'd made love to her. He'd experienced what his dreams had been tormenting him with for weeks. He should be relaxed, satisfied. Instead, his body was tight with need. Rather than easing his hunger for her, making love had only whetted his appetite.

Images raced through his mind. Shadows, deep, reverberating music, her body bathed in moonlight, their frenzied, almost mindless coupling in the darkness.

Mindless.

Realization shot through his brain.

He sat bolt upright in bed. How could he have been so careless? Swinging his legs off the mattress, he rushed across the room, out the door and into the living room.

Heading straight to her room, he lifted his right hand and gave three short, quiet raps on the wood.

She opened it immediately, one finger against kiss-bruised lips. Pushing him back, she eased out of her room and closed the door behind her. "Be quiet, you'll wake her again."

"Laura, I just thought of something," he said, and cursed himself again for being so damn stupid.

"Jeff," she said, "I'm tired and I'd really rather not talk right now—"

No time now for niceties.

"Are you by any chance taking the Pill?" he asked bluntly.

She frowned up at him, then slowly that frown changed to a look of appalled disbelief.

"I take it that means no," he said. He ran one hand across the back of his neck. *More* complications. As if there hadn't already been enough.

"Of course I'm not," she said, wrapping her arms around her waist. Her soft, dewy eyes looked haunted. "It's not as though I had a big use for it up until tonight."

"Damn it," he whispered.

"This doesn't necessarily mean anything," she told him, but it sounded as though she was really reassuring herself. "My chances of actually conceiving have to be slim. It was only the one time."

How many couples, he wondered, had soothed themselves with that particular line over the centuries?

"I should have taken care of it," he said. He *always* took care of it. He'd never believed in trusting one means of birth control alone.

But tonight, for the first time ever, he hadn't taken the time to think. Instead, they'd acted like a couple of kids in the back seat of a car. Now they could have a major problem on their hands.

"This is my fault," he said, even knowing that it was pointless to assign blame. "I'm sorry, Laura."

"Stop it," she said softly but firmly. "I'm a big girl. I should have been looking out for myself."

Then why did he feel so lousy?

"This is getting us nowhere," he told her. "We can't do anything about it now, anyway. When will we know?"

"Hmm?" She shook her head, clearly distracted by the possibilities. "Oh. In another couple of weeks."

He nodded stiffly. Two weeks. Right now, that sounded like an eternity. But look at what had already happened to him in a couple of short weeks. He had been a reasonably carefree bachelor. Now he had a baby, a nanny and possibly *another* baby on the way.

Good Lord.

Looking at the two of them now, no one would guess that less than half an hour ago, they'd been locked in each other's arms. Even though he was standing right in front of her, Jeff felt the distance between them growing with every passing second.

Hoping to bridge the gap before it widened to an impassable chasm, he lifted one hand toward her.

She stepped back, neatly avoiding his touch. Reaching behind her back, she twisted the knob and opened her bedroom door. Pausing briefly, she said, "Good night, Jeff," then she slipped into her room, shutting him out.

He placed his hands on either side of the door frame and leaned forward, scowling into the darkness. What a mess. Jeff sighed and remembered the look on her face just before she closed the door.

If he was any judge, there wouldn't be a repeat of tonight's performance.

Thoroughly disgusted with himself, Jeff gave the closed door one last look, then went back to his empty bed.

The next morning, Laura managed to stay in her room until after Jeff had left for work. Miranda was a bit fretful, but even she cooperated by waiting a little longer than usual for her morning bottle.

As soon as the coast was clear, she hustled to the kitchen, sat the baby down in her high chair and hurriedly prepared Miranda's breakfast.

She was so tired she could hardly keep her eyes open. Of course, that was hardly surprising. She hadn't gotten a wink of sleep all night, what with the images of Jeff darting through her mind...along with the worry that she just might be pregnant.

Laura groaned quietly and reached up to rub her temples. How could she have done something so completely out of character? Not only had she made love with a man she hardly knew, but also she hadn't even *considered* the possibility of a pregnancy.

Only fools and children made that kind of mistake.

And she was no child.

A child. She stopped cold and leaned her forehead on a cabinet door. Please, she prayed silently. She couldn't be pregnant. How could she face her colleagues at school next September? A pregnant, unmarried kindergarten teacher? No, she was sure *that* wouldn't go over well with her principal.

Her eyes squeezed shut on a wave of misery. It wasn't fair. How many times had she dreamed about having children? Ever since she was a girl, she'd longed for a family of her own. When Bill died, she'd put all of those hopes and dreams aside, resigning herself to the fact that she would always be alone.

Now, she very well *might* be pregnant and found herself having to pray frantically that she wasn't.

It could all have been so different, she thought tiredly. If only Bill had lived. Laura kept her eyes firmly closed and tried to draw up a mental image of her former fiancé.

But the once familiar, comforting features blurred and shifted. The harder she tried to focus, the more the images fought her. Faded by the years, her memories of Bill had become distant recollections of warmth.

On the other hand, a vivid portrait of Jeff Ryan leaped into her mind instantly. His eyes, his hands, his mouth as he leaned in to claim a kiss.

Tears filled her eyes as she pushed those mental pictures aside.

Blast you, Bill, she thought angrily. Why did you die? Everything was so much simpler then. So clear. With him, she had known who she was and what she wanted.

With Jeff, everything was different. *She* was different. In ways she would never have expected, she felt herself reacting to him and to the new world she found herself in.

Making love on a couch? With no protection?

That was definitely *not* the old Laura Morgan.

A single tear rolled from the corner of her eye. She caught it with a swipe of her hand and told herself to leave the past in the past. Though she felt safe living with her memories, they offered her no solutions to her current problems. Right now, the present demanded her full attention.

Straightening away from the cabinet, she glanced at the baby, saw that she was happily chewing on the end of the safety strap and smiled softly.

The phone rang while she was stirring baby oatmeal. She grabbed up the receiver, tucked it between her chin and her shoulder and said, "Hello?"

"Hi, Laura," a familiar voice answered. "It's Peggy."

"Peggy," Laura said, glad for the distraction of a friendly voice. "How are you?"

"I'm fine, I wanted to know how *you* were doing."

"I'm sorry," she said, spooning a bit of the cereal into Miranda's open, birdlike mouth. "I should have called you."

"Hey, it's no biggie," her friend countered. "You've been busy."

Busier than she knew, Laura thought with a grimace.

"So what's my new niece like?"

Laura smiled. She couldn't help it. "Right now, she's smearing oatmeal over her face."

Miranda laughed, as if she knew she was being discussed. Smacking both palms down on her high-chair tray, she opened her mouth wide for another mouthful.

"Tell that brother of mine to bring her up for a visit, okay?" Peggy's voice sounded wistful.

"I will," Laura said automatically, then bit her lip before saying, "you know, he still hasn't decided if he's going to keep her or not."

"He'll keep her," Peggy assured her.

"How do you know?"

"I know my brother," Peggy answered, then added to one of her kids, "I said *one* cookie." Speaking to Laura again, she asked, "So, what do you think of Jeff?"

Now, *there* was a loaded question.

"He's..." What? Gorgeous? A wonderful lover? Terrifying? Perhaps the father of her unborn child? She shuddered and settled for "Nice."

"Nice?" Peggy sounded appalled. "That's it? Nice?"

"What did you expect?" Laura said, spooning the last of the oatmeal into Miranda's messy little mouth.

"*Expect* isn't the right word," Peggy told her on a sigh. "*Hoped* would have been more accurate."

Laura picked up a towel, wiped the baby's face, then handed her a bottle. Two chubby fists closed around it and tipped it up.

"Peggy," Laura said, leaning back in the chair.

"You can't blame a girl for trying," Peggy interrupted. "I've thought for the longest time that you and Jeff would be perfect together."

Laura flushed and thanked heaven that her friend couldn't see her face. They had been perfect. More than perfect. But sex wasn't everything.

"Forget it, Peg," Laura said, more for her own benefit than her friend's. She wouldn't fool herself into thinking she and Jeff were madly in love. If she was more attracted to him than was comfortable to admit, no one but *she* had to know that. "I already had my chance at love."

"Please," Peggy groaned. "Don't start telling me about Saint Bill again."

"He was a wonderful man," Laura said hotly, determined now, more than ever, to defend his memory. It was one thing for her to realize that what she and Bill had shared wasn't even close to the chemistry between her and Jeff. It was quite another to let someone else talk about the man she would have married if things had been different.

"I'm sorry. I'm sure he was." There was a long minute of silence before Peggy went on. "But he's gone, honey. And you're still alive. Is it right for you to pack yourself up in mothballs?"

She hadn't been in mothballs. She'd had a life the past eight years. She just hadn't had a man. There was a difference.

"Look," Peggy said, apparently sensing the need for a change of topic. "Tell me about Jeff and the baby. Is he nuts about her?"

Thankful for safe, neutral ground, Laura smiled. "He's so good with her. But he doesn't seem to think so. It's as if he hasn't even noticed how much time he spends with her. And how much he enjoys it."

"Then maybe you should show him."

"What do you mean?"

"I mean," Peggy said, and Laura could hear the grin in her voice, "keep the baby away from him.

Have her asleep by the time he gets home. Make him do without her so that he'll see how much he already loves her. And how much he'd miss her if she was gone."

Not a bad idea, Laura thought. "Okay," she agreed, reaching out to smooth the baby's flyaway hair. "I'll do it. But only because I know what a terrific parent he would be."

"Of course he's good at parenting," Peggy exclaimed. "He's *my* brother, isn't he?" Then in a louder, sterner voice, she ordered, "Teddy, put those scissors down this minute. Don't you *dare* cut your sister's braid off!"

Laura chuckled and wasn't surprised when Peggy said, "Gotta go," and hung up.

Standing up, she pulled Miranda from her high chair and cuddled the messy little person close. "Remember, Miranda," she said, "when you go to visit your cousins, stay clear of Teddy."

Miranda grinned around the nipple in her mouth, and a river of formula ran down her chin.

Jeff opened the door to the apartment, not really sure what kind of a reception he would get. All day, he'd had to balance his duties at work with thoughts of Laura. It hadn't been easy, concentrating on the piles of paperwork he was expected to handle while his brain kept conjuring up images of the night before. Laura in his arms. Laura sighing. Laura crying his name.

Not to mention the image of Laura pregnant.

He'd never been so affected by a woman. He'd

never allowed whatever female he was seeing to invade other aspects of his life. He had always been able to keep his career and his private life separate.

Until now.

Whatever it was between him and Laura, he couldn't allow it to affect his work. They were going to have a talk, whether she wanted to or not. He gritted his teeth and closed the door quietly, telling himself to get a grip. His gaze scanned the inside of the apartment, looking for her. But there was no sign of either Laura or the baby. Irrationally, a hollow emptiness opened in his chest. What if she'd left? What if she had taken the baby and gone?

He knew it was stupid. Laura wouldn't sneak off and she sure as hell wouldn't take the baby if she did.

Still, he was amazed at the sweeping relief he felt when her bedroom door opened and Laura stepped into the living room. She turned, saw him and stopped abruptly. Her gaze met his for an instant before sliding away.

She wore an oversize white T-shirt again and a pair of pale blue shorts, exposing her shapely, lightly tanned legs. He couldn't help wondering what she had on *under* those baggy clothes. That thought brought up the memory of a red lace thong, and his mouth went dry.

For an uncomfortably long minute, he simply looked at her, not sure what to say or where to start.

Ridiculous to feel suddenly tongue-tied.

Jeff tossed his camouflage uniform hat onto the nearby table, then shifted his gaze back to her, willing her to look at him. It didn't work. Finally, he asked, "Where's the baby?"

"Asleep," Laura said, and started for the kitchen.

Asleep? At six o'clock? He checked his watch just to make sure of the time. Normally, Miranda didn't even have her bath until seven-thirty. "Why so early?" he asked, crossing the room to join her.

Laura shrugged. "She seemed tired. Maybe she just didn't get enough sleep last night." Her voice sort of trailed off on the last part of that sentence.

"I know how she feels, then," he said, glad she'd given him an opening.

She ignored him, bent down and pulled a saucepan from the bottom cupboard. "Is soup all right with you?" she asked. "I'm really not very hungry."

"I thought you said you weren't going to cook for me." He deliberately brought back the memory of their first day together, hoping she would smile. She didn't.

"I'm cooking for me," she explained. "There's simply enough for you, too."

"Fine," he said.

"Soup, then." She walked to another cabinet, opened it and stared up at the rows of cans. "Chicken noodle okay?"

"I don't care," he answered impatiently.

She grabbed one can and opened a drawer, rummaging for a can opener.

"Laura," he said.

She didn't even turn around. Just started in on that can of soup as though it were the most important thing in the world.

"Laura, we should talk about last night," he said, still waiting for a response.

"Would you hand me that pan?" she asked.

Grumbling under his breath, he stalked across the small kitchen, grabbed the pan and handed it to her across the table.

"Thanks."

"You're welcome," he said. "About last night…"

"I think it's better if we just pretend last night didn't happen," she said, dumping the condensed soup into the pan. Stepping over to the sink, she filled the can with water, and went back to the stove. As she stirred the mess together, she continued, "It was an accident. Something I'm sure we both regret. Let's go past it, shall we?"

"Go past it." He stared at the back of her head, wishing he could see her expression. Look into her eyes.

"I think that would be best."

"Oh, well…" He nodded sharply, though she couldn't see him, either. He'd wanted to have a reasonable discussion. He'd wanted to have a chance to explain to her that just because the sex had been incredible, it didn't necessarily follow that there would be a relationship between them.

Damn it, *he* had wanted to be the calm, reasonable one.

Briefly, he wondered why he was so upset. Wasn't this just what he'd wanted? Hadn't everything worked out fine?

All day, he'd wondered and worried about a conversation that she had just initiated and ended in about five sentences.

A flicker of anger sparked into life inside him. Who the hell did she think she was, deciding something this important for both of them? The fact that he had been going to do the same thing was irrelevant.

"And what if you're pregnant?" he forced himself to ask. "Do we just go past that, too?"

She went completely still. "We'll worry about that if we have to."

"You can't avoid looking at me forever," he snapped.

Slowly, she turned around to face him. Color stained her cheeks. Her eyes glittered with an emotion he couldn't identify, and her spine was so stiff, she looked as though she might snap in two.

"Happy now?" she asked.

"Delirious." He wasn't sure how to reach her. She seemed more remote now than she had the day she arrived. "Damn it, where is the woman I was with yesterday?" he demanded.

If anything, the splotch of color on her cheeks deepened. "She's gone," Laura said. "Let her go."

"Not yet," he countered grimly. Why was he fighting this? Why was he poking and prodding for a response even though it would be easier for him if she maintained this unbreachable wall around her?

He didn't know. All he knew was that he wanted to see the other Laura again. The Laura who had demanded his passion and given her own.

Coming around the table in a couple of quick steps, he grabbed her upper arms and pulled her close. She tipped her head back to stare up at him. Jeff tried to read the emotions swirling around in her chocolate brown eyes, but they shifted and changed too quickly to be identified.

"I've been thinking about you all day," he admitted, his gaze moving over her features like a dying man looking for signs of heaven. "I couldn't even work. I kept seeing your face, hearing your voice."

"I'm sorry," she said tightly, letting her gaze slide to one side.

He shook her gently. "I don't want an apology," he told her. "I want..."

"What?" she snapped, suddenly breaking free of his grip and taking a step away from him. "What *do* you want?" she repeated. Her voice sounded hollow. Empty.

He looked down at his hands, then let them fall to his sides. Lifting his gaze back to her, he shook his head. "I don't know," he admitted. "But I know I don't want you pretending last night didn't happen. It did, damn it." He reached up and pushed both hands along the sides of his head. "Ignoring it or brushing it under the rug doesn't change anything."

She blinked, opened her mouth, then closed it again.

His reaction didn't even make sense to him. But they had shared something incredible the night before. Something that had touched him more deeply than anything ever had, and he would be damned if he'd let her pretend otherwise.

"Laura," he said, more softly this time, "I know neither one of us *wanted* it to happen..."

She shook her head and bit down on her bottom lip.

"But it did," he went on, determined to reach her. "And I think you felt the same magic I did."

"Magic?" she asked.

"Yeah," he said, taking a cautious step toward her.

"It wasn't magic, Jeff," she corrected, backing away again. "It was lust, pure and simple."

"Lust?" It had been a while since he'd had that word applied to him. The last time, he thought, was when he was sixteen and the father of his prom date had "escorted" him to his car.

"Don't misunderstand," she added while he was still testing the sound of that word in his mind. "I enjoyed it."

He already *knew* she'd enjoyed it.

"But it can't happen again."

He'd been telling himself the same thing all day. Strange that hearing her say it sounded so much more final.

"Laura—"

"I'm not hungry after all," she said thickly. "You can have the soup." Then she turned and scuttled off to her bedroom.

Alone, he didn't move from that spot until he heard the chicken-noodle soup boiling over on the stove.

Eight

Three days later, Laura was hurrying down the short, carpeted hallway toward the apartment. Nearly five o'clock, she thought with a hasty glance at her wristwatch.

Her grip on the stroller handle tightened. She shouldn't have stayed so late at the park. But Miranda had been having so much fun on the baby swings, Laura hadn't had the heart to drag her away from them.

Now, she ran the risk of running into Jeff.

For the past few days, Peggy's idea of keeping the baby away from him had been working fine. By the time he came home from work, Miranda had eaten her dinner and was tucked into bed. In the mornings, the baby had her bath *after* he had left for the base.

The beauty of Peggy's plan was that now, on the

few occasions Laura had spoken with Jeff, he didn't want to talk about their night of lovemaking. Instead, he was peppering her with questions about Miranda. Was she still teething? Did she eat the vegetables she hated so much?

He'd even come home early the night before, trying to catch Miranda still awake. He hadn't succeeded, but Laura was expecting him even earlier tonight.

Halfway down the hall. She hurried her steps a bit, determined to get the baby fed and down for the night before Jeff arrived.

A door on the left opened, and Agnes Butler stepped out of her apartment. Not now, Laura thought. She just didn't have time to listen to another tirade on the dangers of living with Jeff Ryan. Besides being in a hurry, there was that old adage…locking the barn door after the horse was already out and frolicking in the corral.

The older woman, one hand behind her back, scowled at Laura briefly, then bent down to look at the baby. For the past week, Mrs. Butler had managed to catch Miranda and Laura every time they left the apartment. Maybe there was something to Jeff's notion about being spied on.

"Hello, sweet pea," the older woman crooned, and Miranda kicked her feet excitedly against the stroller. "Look what Agnes has for you." Pulling her hand from behind her back, she offered the baby a pastel pink, crocheted, stuffed bunny rabbit.

Miranda babbled incoherently, then grabbed at the toy, immediately stuffing one of the long ears into her mouth.

Stunned by the gesture, Laura stared at the happy

baby for a long moment before turning to study the suddenly surprising woman beside her.

The heavily lined features were softened as she watched the baby, and there was definitely a glint of some undisguised, warm emotion shining in her eyes.

"Agnes Butler," she said thoughtfully, "you're a fraud."

The old woman shot her a sly glance from the corner of her eye. "Don't know what you're talking about," she said.

Laura smiled and shook her head. "Yes, you do," she countered, a chuckle in her voice. "You've got Jeff fooled, you know."

Twin snow-white eyebrows lowered over those sharp blue eyes.

"Me too, until now." Impulsively, she reached out and squeezed the other woman's hand gently, noticing the fragile, papery feel of her skin. "You snap and snarl at everybody, then spend *days* making something like this for a baby you hardly know." She shook her head again. "You know what you are, Agnes?" she asked. *"Kind."*

"Kind." Agnes waved one hand, dismissing the notion entirely. "Nothing kind about it. Feels good to have somebody to do it for. Selfish, really."

"If that's what you call selfish, I can't wait to see your definition of generous."

Agnes sniffed, snatched her hand away and rubbed at the tip of her nose. "You're a nice girl," she said, looking Laura up and down. "And I got to say you're quite the improvement over the sort of females he *used* to bring around here."

Unwillingly, Laura felt a twinge stab at her heart. Which didn't make the least bit of sense. When you're in lust with a person, you don't feel jealousy and envy. For heaven's sake, lust isn't *love*.

"What kind of women?" she asked before she could stop herself.

"Oh, the high-strung type," Agnes said, tipping her nose up with the tip of a finger. "Raw-boned skinny, tight smiles, silk dresses."

Suddenly depressed, Laura glanced down at her own stunning ensemble and grimaced helplessly. A damp, sand-splattered white T-shirt, baggy gray sweat shorts and tennis shoes. And no one would ever call her skinny.

"But haven't seen one of 'em for months," Agnes was saying.

"Months?" Why did that news feel like a bright ray of hope?

"Yeah. Here lately, at least till you came along, keeping my eye on him was about as interestin' as watchin' grass grow."

"I'll try to do better from now on." A deep voice sounded out from right behind Laura.

Blast it, she'd *known* he would be home early today. Instead of turning around to face him, Laura watched Agnes Butler's relaxed, almost friendly features tighten up into a familiar, disapproving mask.

"Anybody ever tell you it's rude to listen in on conversations?" the older woman snapped.

"Not a soul, ma'am," he responded.

"I thought not," she countered.

Laura swiveled her head to look at him as he

stepped up beside her. His lips twitched with the beginnings of a smile as he bantered with Agnes.

"You could teach me manners," Jeff offered.

"I should live as long as that would take," the older woman retorted, then snorted, already turning into her apartment.

"You'll live forever," he assured her.

Agnes stopped. Cocking her head, she glared at him suspiciously over her shoulder. "How do you know?"

He grinned. "Only the good die young."

Agnes sputtered, but Laura noted the spark of humor in her eyes.

"Rude, I tell you. Just plain rude." With that, the old woman closed her door and systematically turned all four locks.

Still surprised by the exchange, Laura stared at the closed door for a long moment of silence before turning to look at Jeff. "She likes you, doesn't she?"

"*Like* is pretty strong," he said, hunkering down to smile at the baby. "*Doesn't hate* is probably closer to the truth."

After ruffling Miranda's hair, Jeff stood up and looked at the woman who continued to haunt his dreams.

"You're home early," she said.

"I have to be these days," he told her. "If I want to catch a glimpse of you or Miranda." Her gaze shifted away from his, but not before he saw a gleam of guilt flash across her brown eyes. "I don't know what you're up to lately, but do you realize that I haven't even *seen* Miranda in days?"

Laura pushed the stroller toward the apartment. "Isn't that the way you wanted it?"

"Wanted what?" he asked as he followed her.

"You didn't want to be bothered by the baby." She dug in her pocket for her set of keys. "I'm seeing to it that you're not."

"Who put you in charge of making Miranda invisible?" Jeff nudged her to one side, unlocked the front door, then opened it, stepping back so she and the stroller could precede him inside.

"You did," she said softly.

"Bull," he countered. "I never said I wanted her hidden away in an attic."

"You don't *have* an attic." Laura shot him a quick look. "But you *did* say that you never wanted kids. That if you had known Hank was going to make you guardian, you would have stopped him."

"That's different. That's how I felt before."

"What's changed?"

He didn't answer. Hell, he wasn't sure *how* to answer.

Shooting a quick glance at the baby, he felt something inside him turn over. She looked as though she'd grown in the past few days. Stupid, he thought. Of course she hadn't grown in a couple of days.

But seeing her felt good. Better than he had thought it would.

It had been a hard thing for him to admit to himself—that he actually missed Miranda. And he didn't think he was up to the challenge of admitting that fact to Laura. Not yet.

Quietly, he closed the front door behind him, automatically turning the door lock.

"What about you?" he asked, watching her.

"What about me?" She bent down to scoop up the baby.

"You've been keeping out of sight, too."

"I've been with the baby," she replied.

A quick answer. Too quick.

"It's more than that," he said. "You've been avoiding me. Deliberately."

She glanced at him covertly, then concentrated on smoothing Miranda's flyaway wisps of hair. "Shouldn't I be?"

"I never said I didn't want a nanny in my life," he stated quietly.

She stilled. A tenuous thread of awareness leaped up between them, practically vibrating in its growing intensity.

"I'm not in your life," she told him, moving for her bedroom with quick, determined strides.

Every step she took hammered at him. It was as if she were walking out of his apartment, distancing herself from him. Jeff couldn't stand the thought of it.

He caught up with her before she could open the door and disappear again. She held Miranda close to her chest, one hand beneath her little bottom, the other splayed protectively across her back.

"You're here, Laura," he said, curling his hands into fists to keep from touching her. "In my home. In my life." The words *In my heart* hovered on his tongue, but he closed his mouth on them.

"Temporarily."

"Now," he corrected.

"Don't do this," Laura pleaded, her voice breaking slightly.

"Do what?" he asked. "Tell you I've missed you? That I dream of you every night and think of you all day?"

She gasped, held the breath trapped in her lungs for a long minute, then released it on a sigh.

"I can't keep my mind on the job," he told her, realizing even as he said it that that was a gross understatement. Hell, the way he'd been feeling lately, the base could have been invaded and he would hardly have noticed.

"Instead," he continued, "all I see is a pair of soft brown eyes—" he reached up and slowly touched the pad of his thumb to her lips "—a completely kissable mouth—" he let his gaze drop to her sand-covered shorts "—and lace-covered skin."

She shivered and he wanted to shout. He knew that she wanted him as badly as he wanted her. He felt it in her. He sensed the heat already building between them.

"Jeff," she said, taking a hasty half step backward, clutching the baby tightly to her. "I..." Clearly, she was reaching for something to say. Something to put him at bay and keep him there. He had no intention of helping her.

She sucked in a deep gulp of air, making a deliberate attempt to steady herself. "You'll have to excuse me," she said stiffly, "I have to bathe the baby and feed her and..."

"I'll do it tonight," he said, already reaching for the baby, who leaned toward him eagerly.

Odd that he should be so willing to take on a task that he had resented in the beginning of his forced fatherhood.

The past few days, he had almost been able to believe that he was again alone in his apartment. He'd had time to himself. Quiet. Uninterrupted peace.

That should have made him happy. Lord knew in the first few days after Miranda's arrival, all he'd done was silently complain about his lost privacy and the burden of responsibility he'd been handed. Now, though, after just a taste of what his life had been like before the baby, he realized that he didn't like it one damn bit.

In fact, he wouldn't have believed this possible a month ago, but he actually missed being a part of something more than just his own life. He missed seeing Miranda and had caught himself wondering about her at odd times of the day. He'd become accustomed to the baby's presence in his life, and her absence had left a void he had never expected to feel.

Miranda's smile made him feel as though he could conquer the world, and her tears broke his heart.

Strangely enough, in a few short weeks, he seemed to have become somebody's daddy.

Miranda's sturdy little body felt right in his arms. The baby laughed up at him and patted his cheek with her grubby fingers. He smiled at her.

Jeff lifted his gaze from the baby to Laura. A fist tightened around his chest, squeezing until he thought drawing a deep breath would be impossible.

Yes, he had missed Miranda.

But he longed for Laura.

Every night, he lay in his bed and listened for the sounds of her moving about her room. He fantasized at work about her oversize sweatshirts and the perfect breasts they hid. His dreams were filled with visions of her, in the silk-and-lace underwear he knew she loved. He remembered every moment of their one night together, and those memories kept his body tight and his temper with co-workers short.

Something had to be done.

"I've missed her," he said softly.

Laura nodded, a film of water glimmering in her eyes.

"I've missed you, too."

Her gaze snapped up to his. "This isn't helping."

"What *would* help, Laura?" he asked, stepping in close to her.

"I don't know that anything can," she said quietly.

"Damn it, why are you making this so hard?" Jeff reached out with one hand, caught her chin with his fingertips and tilted her head up until he could look into the brown eyes that seemed to be deeper and more velvety every time he saw them. "It doesn't have to be."

"Of course it does," she said with a slow shake of her head. "Neither of us planned on this happening."

Plans. She surely was big on plans. But then, he admitted silently, he used to be, too. Until about fifteen pounds of female trouble had landed in his lap and shattered any sense of planning that he'd ever done.

Suddenly, something Laura'd said to him the night

they had made love came back to him, and in the next instant, he heard himself tossing her words back at her.

"Didn't you tell me that plans don't always work out? That life has a way of just happening?" Her gaze shifted from his. He went on. "You said you had to adapt. To adjust."

"This is different," she protested, her voice husky as it scraped past her throat.

"How?"

She shook her head, apparently unable to come up with a valid reason. Hurriedly, Jeff pushed on.

"I've wanted you, Laura," he said, willing her to hear the hunger in his voice. "I dream about holding you again. Burying myself inside you. Feeling your heartbeat thundering against my chest."

She dragged in a long, shaky breath and slowly lifted her gaze to meet his.

She was weakening; he could feel it. Desire roared through him.

"Tonight, Laura," he demanded, and congratulated himself on making his voice work despite the knot of need lodged in his throat. "Give me tonight, and we'll let tomorrow take care of itself."

Her breathing quickened and shallowed out. Her teeth pulled nervously at her bottom lip.

A long moment passed, and Jeff wondered desperately if he'd pushed too hard, or not enough. He was only certain of one thing. He couldn't spend another long, lonely night with her so close and yet so far away.

He needed her, damn it.

"It's a mistake," she whispered.

"It's inevitable," he countered.

"We shouldn't," she said.

"But we will?"

"Yes," she agreed helplessly. "We will."

By the time Miranda was bathed, fed and put down to sleep, Laura's nerves were as tightly strung as piano wire. Her stomach pitched and rolled constantly, and a low, burning ache had settled at her center, reminding her of what was coming.

She flipped the faucets on and turned the handles until the stream of water rushing from the showerhead was just the right temperature.

The small bathroom filled with steam slowly. It crept from behind the edge of the white shower curtain and swirled over the tiled floor like warm fog. Then it lifted in a slow, writhing dance, twisting around her calves and thighs as it reached for the ceiling.

Laura stared into the mirror as she pinned her hair up on top of her head. Her gaze slipped over her reflection idly, and she couldn't help wondering what Jeff found so appealing about her figure. Her breasts were too small to be voluptuous, her hips too rounded to be fashionable, and she would never have a small waist. Her legs were her best feature, and they were far too short.

Self-consciously, she wrapped her arms around her middle and wasn't surprised to find that her hands were cold, despite the rising, damp heat in the bathroom.

She shouldn't have agreed to this, she told herself sternly. She should have been strong. She should have told him that adding to their first mistake would only compound the problem.

Instantly, visions of their time on the couch raced through her mind, and her nipples tightened in anticipation. She groaned quietly and admitted that it was pointless to fight it. Whatever attraction lay between her and Jeff, it was too strong to ignore.

Sighing, she turned, stepped into the tub and drew the curtain closed behind her. She moved beneath the spray of water, letting it pour onto her face and chest. The hot, stinging, needlelike drops pelted her skin and teased her already raw nerve endings.

Snatching the bar of soap, she rubbed it between her palms, working up a good lather before applying the suds to her shoulders and neck.

"Can I do your back?" a deep, rumbling voice penetrated the steamy wall surrounding her, and Laura jumped, startled.

"Go away," she ordered, instinctively keeping her back to him as he drew the curtain aside and stepped over the rim to join her beneath the rush of hot water.

One of his hands touched her shoulder and slowly, lazily drifted along her spine to her behind.

Laura shivered.

"We both want to take a shower," he said, the rumble of his voice echoing in the small room. "Why not save water while we're at it?"

Laura groaned inwardly. It was one thing to make love to a man in the dark shadows of a bedroom—or a living room—she qualified silently. It was quite another to stand in the bright fluorescent light of a bathroom and have him share a shower in a tub that seemed to be shrinking by the second.

"Laura?" he said softly.

She shot him a quick, backward glance and knew immediately that she was sunk.

Clouds of steam wound around his head. Pale blue eyes shimmering with the heat of desire watched her. Droplets of water clung to the faint brush of dark blond hair that dusted his broad chest. Her gaze dropped farther, landing on the hard, thick proof of the need he felt for her.

"Hand me the soap," he coaxed.

Wordlessly, she did as he asked. She watched as he worked up a lather, then held her breath as he reached for her.

His strong hands fell on her shoulders. His fingers rubbed at either side of her neck, and she felt her muscles liquefy as he gently eased away the tight knots of tension.

Laura leaned forward, resting her forehead on the cool, wet, tiled wall and concentrated on the feel of his hands. Soapy lather made his skin glide along hers, down the length of her spinal column to the curve of her bottom.

His palms cupped her behind, caressing and kneading the tender flesh until she moaned with pleasure and leaned more heavily against the wall. Her right hand gripped the porcelain soap dish bolted to the tiles and her knuckles whitened with the effort to hold herself erect as he continued exploring her body.

"Lovely," he murmured in a husky voice pitched just above the rush of the water. "So lovely."

Her knees wobbled, and she stiffened, locking them into position. She absolutely refused to dissolve into a mass of sensation at his feet.

Then one of his soap-covered hands dipped between her legs, urging them to part for him. The soft, slick feel of his fingers on her thighs brought another gasp and a low, throaty moan from her. Laura pressed herself fully against the blue-and-white tiles, turned her face to one side and closed her eyes.

"Let me touch you, Laura," he whispered.

Instantly, she opened her thighs, widening her already precarious stance on the slippery tub floor. Her breath quickened. Her stomach tightened, and her mouth went dry. Holding on to the soap dish for dear life, she waited for the intimate caress she knew was coming.

Then he kissed the back of her neck.

Laura jolted as electricity sizzled along her nerve endings. His lips and tongue teased her nape before moving down, along her spine. Gooseflesh leaped up on her skin and raced across her body in his wake.

"Jeff," she murmured, and tasted the sweetness of his name on her lips.

She felt him kneel behind her and wanted to protest, but the words wouldn't come. His long, soapy, slick fingers rubbed and smoothed skin that had become so sensitive, she trembled at each touch.

One of his hands slipped between her thighs from behind, and she tensed, everything within her coiled tightly in anticipation. He dipped two fingers into her liquid heat, stroking and pressing against her internal muscles until her entire body was a quivering mass of sensation.

She groaned brokenly and spread her legs farther in a greedy attempt to feel more of him. The still rising steam held her in its foggy grasp, surrounding her with damp heat and blinding her to all but the mist and Jeff's touch.

Then he kissed her bottom, raking his teeth across the tender flesh gently but firmly. Slowly, he stood up, rubbing the length of his body along hers. His thickened groin prodded at her, reminding her that there was more to come.

Laura's breath caught in her chest. Her heart slammed against her ribs in a wild, unsteady beat. Her knees trembled. Her grip on the soap dish tightened even further.

When he had his front firmly pressed to her back, he pulled his hand free of her body, despite the slight whimpering noise that escaped her at his desertion.

But he didn't move away. Instead, he slid his right hand around to the front of her, down over her abdomen and past the triangle of curls at the apex of her thighs.

Grateful and eager, Laura whispered, "Yes, Jeff. Oh, please, now."

He bent his head to kiss her cheek, the corner of her mouth. She couldn't move. Dared not inch away from the tiled wall that had become her only support now that her limbs were useless to her.

As his hand smoothed along her wet flesh to cup her hot, throbbing center, she shivered violently. His thumb brushed across a hardened nub of desire. He whispered to her, his words lost in the rush of water and the pounding of her heart. Her hips moved frantically as he pushed her relentlessly along a path she had thought never to wander again.

Her body bucking against his hands, she twisted this way and that, desperately seeking a release that seemed to hover just out of reach. Jeff moved even closer to her, aligning his body to hers.

Breathing labored, she gasped for air in the tiny, steam-filled enclosure. Helpless to do anything but ride the incredible wave of pleasure just peaking within her, Laura shouted his name as the first explosion took her over the edge.

Nine

His hands shaking, Jeff shut off the water, and stepped out of the tub. He turned and pulled Laura into his arms. She sagged against him, her body still trembling as she sighed his name. He didn't bother to grab towels. He wanted her now. Wet and flushed from the steam. Silently, he headed for his bedroom.

He'd wanted to make love to her in the shower. Watching her as a climax tore through her had shaken him to his soul and pushed his control to its limits.

But he wouldn't make another mistake with her. This time, he would show her the care he should have used their first time together.

Entering the dark bedroom, he walked directly to the bed and laid her down atop the fresh white sheets. She stretched languidly, opened her eyes and smiled up at him. Wet tendrils of her hair snaked out in a star-burst around her head. Her eyes were clouded with the fresh memories of her passion.

She whispered his name and lifted her arms toward him.

He gritted his teeth, yanked the bedside table drawer open and fumbled in its contents blindly. After a long moment, he found what he needed, picked up the foil packet, then slammed the drawer shut again.

His fingers, suddenly clumsy, tore at the wrapper.

"Jeff," she said softly, and came up on one elbow, her free hand held out toward him. "Let me."

He sucked in a gulp of air, incredibly aroused at just the thought of her hands on him. Deliberately, he steadied himself and handed her the packet.

Laura sat up and scooted closer to the edge of the bed. Jeff's breath came in short, shallow puffs. He watched her pull the cream-colored latex free of its wrapping, then held his breath as she reached for him.

Her fingers closed around him tightly. Her thumb stroked the underside of his shaft, and he surged forward, into her grasp, just managing to muffle a groan aching in his throat.

"Laura," he said tightly. "I'm walking a real fine edge here."

She smiled, a knowing, completely feminine curving of her lips. Leaning into him, she kissed his belly, and jagged spears of heat sliced through him. He muttered a curse as more of his control fell away.

"Jump off that edge, Jeff," she urged him softly.

He looked down at her and felt his heart stop. Her mouth just a breath away from his rigid arousal, she leaned in even closer. His teeth ground together. His hands curled into fists as if searching for something—anything—to grab hold of. The only possible way for him to maintain his too ragged sense of self-control would be for him to close his eyes.

Yet he couldn't look away.

He watched her lips touch him. Felt the soft hush of her breath caress his hardened flesh.

A low rumble of need escaped him. Her damp hair against his thighs served as a dramatic contrast to the fire she had started elsewhere. A moment. Two. He luxuriated in her intimate touch and at the same time craved to be inside her. To be buried so deeply within her that they would never be truly apart again.

Suddenly, Jeff couldn't stand it anymore. Reaching for her, he set his hands at either side of her head and tipped her face up to his. When their eyes met, he was humbled and rocked to his core by the raw emotion he read in her gaze.

Through tightly gritted teeth, he said, "Put the condom on me, Laura. I need to be inside you and I can't wait much longer."

"I need that, too, Jeff," she told him, though her voice was thin and wavering. "More than I thought possible."

"Hurry, Laura," he urged. "Hurry."

Her fingers stretched the latex and slowly, carefully, rolled the shield down over his length. Its tightness bit into his flesh, but any discomfort was wiped away by the knowledge that this was his only means of protecting her. Cherishing her.

She scooted back on the mattress, stretched out and parted her thighs. Then she reached for him, arms wide in welcome. He couldn't wait another moment. The sweet torment had already gone on too long. A wild need burned in him now with an energy that wouldn't be denied.

He knelt between her thighs, slid his hands beneath her bottom and lifted her hips slightly for his entry. As he pushed himself into her warmth, he paused, reveling in the feel of her closing around him. Even shielded from her, he experienced the same overpowering sensation he had the first time.

It was like coming home.

With his next breath, he thrust deeply inside her, satisfaction rippling through his bloodstream. In seconds, an ancient rhythm claimed him and drove him on relentlessly.

Laura's hands clutched at his shoulders and forearms. He felt her short fingernails digging into his flesh. He leaned over her, bending his head to claim first one rigid nipple and then the other. His tongue rolled across the tender flesh, drawing it deeply into his mouth. He suckled her, working her flesh with his lips and tongue until she writhed and twisted beneath him.

Her hands moved to his chest. He felt her fingertips brush across his flat nipples, and a bolt of lightning shot through him. He redoubled his efforts at her breasts, lavishing his attentions on them, each in turn.

"Please, Jeff," she whispered. "It feels too good." She shook her head against the sheets, her hair spread out and around her shoulders. "I can't do this again. It's too soon."

"Again," he muttered thickly. And again, he

thought, lost in the sensations she brought him. Caught in the web of her scent, her taste.

Despite her protests, her hips rose and fell in tandem with his. He felt the change in her as another tearing climax approached. Her breathing sped up and she drew one ragged breath after another. She raked her fingernails down his chest, around his waist and then up his back.

He lifted his head and drove himself into her, pushing them both higher, faster than they had gone before.

Jeff looked down into her face and watched her features tighten as she strained to reach the goal that came closer with each of his powerful thrusts.

Her legs came up and wrapped around his hips. She pulled him deeper, closer. Her back arched, she tipped her head back into the mattress and cried out brokenly. He set his hands at either side of her head and bent over her, claiming her mouth as the pleasure took her, rocked her.

As her trembling eased, his own release rushed through him. He parted her lips with his tongue and took her breath for his as he shuddered in her arms.

He rolled to one side, keeping one arm around her and drawing her close. She snuggled into his warmth, using the last of her strength to lay one arm across his chest so she could feel the steady, thunderous beat of his heart.

Laura's own heartbeat slowed, and the wild sizzle in her veins gradually dimmed to a low hum of satisfaction. She drew a deep breath and let it shudder out of her lungs. If she had had to run for her life at the moment, she would be in big trouble. Every muscle in her body was limp. Even her bones felt as if they had turned to mush.

Jeff's fingertips dusted across her back. Laura smiled sadly, regretfully. His gentle touch twisted a silken cord of tenderness around her heart. She didn't want to acknowledge it. Couldn't bring herself to admit to any feelings beyond contentment. To do that would be to invite disaster.

Her chest tightened with an overwhelming emotion she refused to name, even to herself.

A film of tears blurred her vision suddenly, and she closed her eyes against a pain she knew would eventually assert itself. Nestling her head into the hollow of his shoulder, Laura closed her mind, shutting off the thoughts that threatened to ruin this one beautiful moment.

For now, she only wanted to rest in his arms and listen to the heartbeat of the man who had become too important to her.

A soft sound of distress woke him from a sound sleep. Jeff stared at the ceiling for a long moment, trying to figure out just what he'd heard.

Laura sighed and moved in closer to him. Her head on his chest, her warm breath brushed across his skin like a whisper. He smiled into the darkness and pressed the memory of this moment deeply into his brain. The silky texture of her skin. The warmth of her body curved into his. The sensual drape of her unbound hair spilling across his arm.

He committed all of those senses to memory. Fifty years from now, he wanted to be holding her just like this and be able to reach back in time and relive their beginning.

He stopped, stunned at the thought. His smile faded as he tried to shy away from it, but it was too late. It was as if his subconscious had already accepted the fact that he and Laura would be together forever.

Before he could wrestle with his own feelings, the sound that had awakened him came again. A thin, mewling cry that tugged at his heart.

Miranda.

He looked down at the sleeping woman in his arms and smiled to himself. He wouldn't wake her. No reason for both of them to have their dreams interrupted. Carefully, Jeff slipped from under Laura's outflung arm and eased off the mattress. Pausing long enough to grab his robe from a nearby chair and tug it on, he started for the open doorway.

Darkness didn't slow his steps. He could find his way safely through the apartment even if blindfolded. At the door of his room, though, he paused for a brief glance at Laura.

Even the deep shadows couldn't keep him from seeing her. Her form neatly outlined against the plain white sheets, she slid her arm across the mattress as if searching for him in her sleep.

How perfect she looked in his bed.

How good she felt in his life.

Vaguely, he wondered how he had lived as long as he had without her. And how he would ever survive when she left him at the end of the summer.

Jeff brushed one hand across the top of his head, then scowling, tugged the belt of his robe tighter around his waist. A moment later, he turned his back on Laura and headed off to the other bedroom.

Slivers of moonlight pierced the darkness, pointing the way to the crib, where Miranda lay fretting, her blankets twisted around her legs. Jeff stared down at her for a long minute. She rubbed her eyes with two little fists and squirmed uncomfortably, her tiny mouth forming a pout in her sleep.

Jeff reached across the crib rail and gently released her from her cocoon. Immediately, Miranda flipped onto her side, dragged the stuffed bunny close and drifted back into her dreams.

In the hush of darkness, the baby's deep, even breathing measured the passing seconds. Leaning his forearms on the rail, he stared down at the child who had changed his life in so many ways.

Shaking his head softly, he realized just how small, innocent…defenseless she really was.

Something tightened in his chest, threatening to strangle his heart. There were so many things in the world for her to explore, discover. Joy. Pain. Love.

He reached into the crib again and gently ran his fingers along her cheek. Her mouth worked frantically, as if she were sucking on a bottle filled with her favorite drink.

That silly pink bunny stared up at him through wide, green-yarn eyes. Another change wrought by Miranda. Who would have guessed that Agnes Butler had such a soft spot for babies?

He shook his head slowly. "Why should that surprise me, though?" he asked in a whisper. "Look what you managed to do to me."

Miranda slept on, unaware of the man talking to her.

"I never wanted kids, you know," he confessed. "But you probably guessed that early on." He pulled her blanket a bit higher up on her shoulders. "Didn't seem to stop you any, though. You kept right on, looking cute and smiling at me. Expecting me to fall into line." He chuckled gently. "Just like a woman. Sneak under a man's defenses. Change his life until he can't remember what the world was like without you and then reel him in."

His smile slowly disappeared as he sunk down to kneel on one knee beside her crib. At eye level with her, he stared at Miranda, captivated by the sweep of eyelashes across her cheeks and by the tiny mouth, still working in her sleep.

Love blossomed in his chest, swelling and growing to painful proportions. He was good and caught, he thought. He couldn't give her up. This tiny baby had become an integral part of his life. He couldn't imagine not being around to see her take her first steps. Hear her first word.

The realization that had been building within him for weeks reared up and demanded to be acknowledged.

There would be no neat adoption.

He wouldn't be calling child welfare, looking for a way out. Where Miranda was concerned, he thought with a smile, there was no way out.

He swallowed hard and began whispering again, forcing the words past a tight throat.

"I'm no prize, Miranda," Jeff said. "I don't know much about being a father. I'll probably make lots of mistakes, too." She should be warned about just what she was letting herself in for, he told himself. "But I promise you, I'll try." He reached through the bars of her crib and curved the palm of his hand gently around the back of her head.

Inhaling sharply, he blew it out in a rush and added, "I love you, Miranda." He smiled, feeling the relief at finally admitting to the emotion that had been plaguing him constantly. "Believe me, I'm just as surprised as you are. I didn't count on this happening. Heck, I would have bet money on it never happening to me."

He shrugged and chuckled quietly. "But if I've learned anything since you first came to me, it's that life *does* change when you least expect it. You and Laura both taught me that," he said. "I can't even imagine my life without you two in it," he admitted, his voice tinged with the wonder he felt at that one simple fact.

The baby shifted, cooed something unintelligible and turned her face into his touch.

Jeff's breath caught. He felt the responsibility of her care settle on his shoulders, and amazement flooded him as he realized that it didn't feel at all like a burden. More like a blessing.

His vision blurred suddenly and he blinked to clear it. "I promise you, Miranda," he said softly, "I will do everything in my power to keep you and to make sure you're happy. I may not be much of a daddy yet, but you can work on me." He paused thoughtfully. "Daddy. Sounds kind of nice, doesn't it?"

One corner of his mouth lifted and a protective pride rose in his chest. "But there is one thing you should know right off, for when you get older,'' he said sternly. ''There'll be no boys hanging around the house. Since no one will ever be good enough for you anyway, I don't want a bunch of teenage Don Juan's coming after my baby.''

She sniffed, rubbed her tiny nose and made a grab for her bunny again.

Slowly, Jeff stood up and stared down at her. ''My baby,'' he repeated, liking the sound of it. ''My little girl.''

Laura swiped at the tears coursing down her cheeks.

Standing in the shadowed darkness of the living room, wearing only one of Jeff's camouflage uniform shirts, she kept to the side of the doorway where she could hear him and not risk being seen. Quickly, she glanced into the room and saw him leaning over the crib as he made heartfelt promises to a baby he had grown to love.

Laura straightened up again and struggled to control the rising tide of tenderness washing over her. His words had reached into her heart and opened up all the dark corners she had lived with for too long.

She ached to go to him, lay her head on his chest and feel his arms close around her. At that moment, there was nothing she wanted more than to experience the warm safety she found in the circle of his embrace.

But Laura didn't move. Not only because she didn't want him to know she had again eavesdropped on him as he spoke to Miranda. But also because of something he had said about her.

He couldn't imagine his life without her.

Did that mean he loved her, too?

A sense of panic shot through her bloodstream, obliterating the tender feelings and the overpowering longing she felt for him.

She ran her palms up and down her arms, feeling the rough fabric of his shirt scrape against her skin. His scent clung to the material, teasing her with every breath she took.

A sudden chill crept along her flesh.

This couldn't work. Her own fears would defeat her. Whatever it was that lay between them was destined to fail. She'd known that all along. Ever since the first time she'd kissed him.

Another tear trickled from the corner of her eye, and she quickly brushed it away.

She couldn't stay much longer, she told herself. She couldn't be around him as he made plans for his and Miranda's future. A future Laura could have no part in.

Briefly, her mind drew up an image of the long, lonely years stretching out ahead of her. She pictured the faceless woman who would replace her in Miranda's life. Would that same stranger take her place with Jeff, as well?

Would he and Miranda forget all about her once she was gone?

A sharp stab of regret pierced her heart at the thought.

But there was nothing she could do about it. Nothing at all, beyond enjoying whatever time she had left with the two people she'd come to care for so deeply.

Pulling in a series of deep, ragged breaths, she scuttled back to his bedroom and crawled onto the mattress. Laura reluctantly took off his shirt, tossed it to the floor and lay down, drawing the sheet up over her.

If she was very lucky, by the time he came back to bed, she would be asleep.

Ten

Born under a lucky star she wasn't.

Laura could have feigned sleep, but the truth was, she didn't want to. What she wanted was to feel Jeff's arms slide around her, listen to his heartbeat and content herself with the moment.

He settled himself against the pillows, and when she moved up close to him, he wrapped one arm around her and held her tightly to his side.

"Everything all right?" she whispered, despite knowing that all was well.

"Yeah," he said, his tone as hushed as hers. "She's asleep again."

"Good."

"I'm going to keep her, Laura. Raise her as my own."

Despite the situation, she smiled and kissed his chest. "I knew you would."

He chuckled, and she felt the rumbling sound beneath her cheek.

"Then you knew more than I did," he said.

"You should always bear that in mind," Laura countered, striving desperately for a light, teasing note.

"Laura—" he tightened his hold on her as if expecting her to dart away from him "—there's something else. Something I want to talk to you about."

Panic opened up inside her. The darkness seemed to creep closer, threatening to swallow her. She couldn't let him talk. The serious tone of his voice warned her that whatever it was he wanted to say…she couldn't allow herself to hear it.

She lifted her head and looked up at him. His gaze, soft and warm, was locked on her. "Not tonight," she whispered, and she heard the plea in her voice. "No more talking tonight."

"But…" He lifted one hand and smoothed her hair back from her face.

"Please," she whispered, turning into his touch and dropping a quick kiss in the center of his palm. Sliding up over him, Laura bent her head to kiss him, giving him everything she could.

Everything she dared risk.

Jeff rolled over, flipping her onto her back. His hands glided over her skin as he traced her curves with questing fingers. The magic that lay between them burst into glorious life, splintering the darkness with brilliant shards of color and light.

Staring down into her liquid brown eyes, he at last

realized the depth of the love he felt for her. It both terrified and amazed him.

He wasn't sure when it had happened, not that it made a difference. All that mattered was that he had actually been granted something that he had long since decided would never be his.

Passion, desire, love, swept through his bloodstream, carrying him to a place just short of madness. He wanted to say the words out loud and savor the taste of them. And he wanted to make her admit to loving him, too. He knew she did. He felt it every time she touched him. He heard it in her voice and sensed it in her caresses.

But as he continued to look into those incredible eyes of hers, he reluctantly accepted the fact that she clearly wasn't ready. Hadn't she hidden from him for days after the first time they'd made love? For what reason if not to hide from the depth of her emotions?

He would have to wait. Wait until she was as sure of this new love as he was.

Disappointment was relieved by the knowledge that he had until the end of summer to convince her.

He wouldn't lose her.

Not now. Not after finally realizing what he had found with her.

Laura lifted one hand and pulled his head down to hers. Thoughts and plans for the future dissolved as he gave himself over to the present and the joy of loving her.

In an effort to keep her sanity and quiet her mind, the next morning, Laura went shopping. She had Miranda dressed, in her stroller and out the front door early enough to be on the spot when the stores opened.

It wasn't that she needed or even *wanted* anything in particular. But she knew she couldn't sit in that apartment all day with nothing but an infant and her own thoughts for company.

She needed open spaces. She needed to feel the wind in her face. She needed to walk off some of the nervous energy that had been pumping through her body since the night before.

Since she had overheard Jeff's plans for the future and realized that she couldn't be a part of them.

Instantly, she recalled the determined look on his face when he had come back to bed. Every instinct she possessed had screamed at her that he was about to make a proposal. A proposal she would have had to reject. She couldn't risk love again. The pain of loss cut too deep. Thankfully, she had managed to keep him from saying the words that would have ended their time together. For now.

Her fingers curled around the stroller handle, squeezing it tightly. Laura wasn't sure just how much longer she could bear to stay, pretending to be a member of this little family. She would never be able to last out the summer though; that much she was sure of.

The sleepy coastal town was small, with more touristy stores than general merchandise, but Laura hardly noticed. She and Miranda browsed through craft stores, card shops and in a baby boutique, Laura purchased a sweet romper and sun bonnet for Miranda.

Afterward, they stopped at a coffee house for a well-deserved break of formula and lattes.

Finally, window shopping on their way back to the apartment, Laura stopped dead in front of a small ladies' clothing store.

Sunshine sparkled on the clean glass and danced across the scrolled letters spelling out Francine's Finery. But Laura wasn't admiring the well-clothed mannequin in the window or trying to see past the glare into the shop.

Instead, her attention was caught by her own reflection. She tightened her grip on the stroller handle reflexively as she studied the woman she had become.

Somehow, she'd never actually paid much attention before now. The woman in the glass looked at least ten years older than thirty. Hair in an untidy ponytail, figure hidden beneath a baggy yellow tunic top and a calf-length full skirt that ballooned around her in the breeze. Even her shoes looked matronly. Sensible loafers, no stockings.

Lifting her gaze back up to meet her reflected eyes, she stared at a woman who suddenly seemed like a stranger.

"What have you done to yourself?" she whispered, and lifted one hand to smooth back a wild strand of hair, plucked free by the wind.

She used to be cute.

Okay, maybe not cute. But *interesting* looking, certainly. What had happened? Even as her mind posed the question though, she knew the answer.

Bill's death had happened.

Laura lifted one hand from the stroller and plucked

at her too large shirt. Teeth worrying her bottom lip, she admitted that right after Bill's accident, she had gone into hiding. Oh, she hadn't locked herself away in a tower somewhere. It might have been healthier if she had. At least then she would have been forced to go out once in a while, if only for food.

But no. She'd built a tower around herself. She'd hidden away behind baggy clothes and messy hair. Hiding from the pain of loving and then losing someone, she had also been hiding from the world. She had thought that by dressing like a ragpicker and avoiding makeup and a decent hairstyle, she would be able to keep any man from becoming interested. She hadn't wanted to risk feeling again. Loving again.

"The joke's on you," she told the woman in the glass. "It didn't work."

Jeff had seen through the frumpy exterior she offered the world, to the woman she really was. Somehow, he had touched her soul despite the safeguards she had erected so carefully.

Now the sad clothing she wore didn't represent anything but bad taste.

Although she couldn't allow herself to be in love again, there was no longer any reason to hide behind ill-fitting clothes.

"Well," she said thoughtfully, with a glance at the baby in the stroller, "since frumpery didn't help anyway, why don't we go inside and see if we can find something that suits me better?"

Miranda kicked her feet and squirmed excitedly.

"You're right," Laura said, determinedly steering the stroller toward the front door. "I believe it's time for the real me to rejoin the world. A little bit at a time.''

He stepped into the apartment and paused to take a deep, appreciative whiff of the delicious aromas drifting out of the kitchen.

Man, how things changed. Only a few weeks ago, he would have been coming home to an empty apartment, a microwavable dinner and maybe a rented movie.

Domestic bliss. Who knew it would feel so good?

From the kitchen came Miranda's garbled attempts at talking and the distinct sound of Laura, singing.

Grinning, he tossed his hat onto the table and started across the room. In the entryway, he stopped dead.

''Hi,'' Laura said. ''I didn't hear you come in.''

Stunned, Jeff's gaze swept over her from head to toe and back again. The transformation started with her hair. She'd had it trimmed, and now it lay neatly just above her shoulders in a soft wave that tempted him even from across the room to run his fingers through it. But she hadn't stopped with her hairdo.

She wore a pale peach tank top, its thin, delicate fabric caressing and outlining the swell of her breasts. The hem of that shirt came to an abrupt end just above her waist, giving him a tantalizing glimpse of skin. Pastel yellow shorts clung to her hips and thighs, with the determined grip of a lover's hands, displaying every curve with detailed precision.

Shaking his head, Jeff rubbed his suddenly dry mouth and muttered a fervent ''Wow.''

Laura's smile warmed him. ''Thanks,'' she said.

"What's the occasion for the shopping trip?" he asked, wondering why all of a sudden she had come out from under wraps, so to speak.

"No occasion," she told him, and tore the lettuce into salad-size bites. "I just decided it was time."

"I approve," he said, in a gross understatement.

"Good," she told him. "Now, you're just in time to set the table."

Smiling, he bent down, kissed the top of Miranda's head, then walked to the cabinet where the plates were kept.

He hadn't been able to take his eyes off of her all through dinner. Hell, Jeff thought, if someone asked him what he had just eaten, he couldn't have said. For all he'd tasted of it, it might as well have been sawdust.

From the moment he'd seen her in those new clothes, he'd felt hope shimmering through him. There had to be a reason for her abrupt shift from frump to fashion plate. He couldn't help thinking that maybe it wasn't just a new wardrobe she was in the market for. But a new life, as well.

A life with him.

"Do you smell something?" Laura asked suddenly, wrinkling her nose.

"What?" It took him a moment to come back from his daydreams. He sniffed the air and frowned. Definitely something burning. Glancing behind her, he asked, "Did you leave a burner on accidentally?"

"No," she said, but dutifully got up, walked to the

stove and checked anyway. She shook her head as she looked at him.

He pushed up from his chair and walked quickly around the apartment. Odd. The smell seemed to get stronger the closer he moved to the front door. That couldn't be right.

Then he heard it.

A shriek of sound, muffled but distinct. Almost like a— Realization dawned with the impact of a bullet.

Reacting instantly, he shouted, "Smoke alarm downstairs. There's a fire." He reached the kitchen in a few short strides and snatched Miranda from her high chair. The baby yelped at such abrupt treatment, but he couldn't take the time to reassure her.

Old but not forgotten feelings surged in his bloodstream. A strange mixture of terror and calm, panic and logic asserted itself in his brain. As if he were on a battlefield again, he took charge, already planning the best way for his troops—now his family—to survive.

His gaze shot to Laura. He saw her cheeks pale and watched her brown eyes widen in alarm. Immediately, he snapped, "Don't panic." He waited for her gaze to clear as she looked at him. Only then did he continue. "We probably have lots of time. Let's just get outside. *Now.*"

She jerked him a stiff nod, then turned, not for the front door, but for her bedroom.

"Where the hell are you going?" he demanded.

"To get Miranda's jacket."

"Forget the damn jacket," he told her, taking the few steps that separated her from him. Grabbing hold of her arm, he started dragging her toward the only exit. "Get out of the building—that's all that's important."

Clutching Miranda to his chest, despite her struggles to get free, Jeff stopped at the door and took the time to touch his palm to the wooden panel. Cool. He breathed an inward sigh of relief. At least he knew there wasn't a wall of fire in the hallway, waiting to engulf them.

He twisted the knob, poked his head out the opening to check the situation, then stepped into the hall. "Come on," he said to Laura.

She moved out to stand beside him and reached for the baby.

"I'll carry her," he said, his tone brooking no arguments. "You stay behind me. Take hold of my belt and don't let go." No matter what else happened, he didn't want to take the chance of losing her. If she was holding on to him, he would know where she was at all times.

They passed Agnes Butler's door, and he stopped long enough to pound on it. "Agnes!" he shouted, then paused to listen for an answer. When none came, he told himself she was already outside. He couldn't wait. His instincts told him to get his Laura and Miranda to safety quickly.

The door of the only other apartment on the top floor stood open. Apparently, that tenant hadn't even bothered to close his door on the way out.

Jeff kept going along the carpeted runner. Strange, he didn't remember the hall being this long before. It seemed to be taking forever to reach the stairs.

His gaze narrowed sharply. At the end of the hall, just past the elevator, a tentacle of smoke reached the head of the stairs.

His chest tightened. His mouth went dry.

The ribbon of gray mist curled and twisted on the ceiling before sidling farther down the hall, toward them. The shrill bleat of the smoke alarm was louder now and sounded like the screams of the damned.

Ignoring the whisper of fear rattling around in his head, Jeff hurried his steps, forcing himself to lead his family into the smoke. There was no other way. They couldn't take the elevator. They had to use the stairs.

"Jeff," Laura said tightly, "the baby. She'll choke."

The smoke was at eye level now and falling with every passing second. Soon none of them would be able to draw a breath without gasping.

"She'll be all right," he answered, then he shifted Miranda so that her small face was turned into his chest. He cupped the back of her head, holding her in place. She'd still be able to breathe, but hopefully she wouldn't take in much smoke. "Stay down," he said. "Keep low." They hunched their shoulders, trying to keep their faces below the dropping gray curtain. "Okay," he told her. "Let's go."

They plunged down the stairs, their bodies slicing through the wisps of smoke, tearing it into strips that writhed around them like ghostly ropes, trying to hold them back. Keep them inside.

The front door stood open, and Jeff made right for it.

On the lawn, people from all over the street were

gathered. A surfer and a middle-aged businessman type had garden hoses in their hands, the streams of water aimed through the windows of one of the three apartments on the ground floor.

Down the four short steps to the grass, and still he didn't stop. Not until he had Laura and Miranda a safe distance from the fire that had threatened everything he held dear.

Under the heavy limbs of a gnarled maple tree, he released Miranda from his stranglehold and laughed when she made a face and howled her displeasure. She sounded wonderful. In the next instant, he half turned, pulling Laura into the circle of his arms, while still juggling an infuriated infant.

"All right?" he asked, dipping his head to plant a kiss on Laura's forehead.

"Yeah," she answered, tipping her face up to his, showing him a small, frightened smile.

She was breathing heavily, and her eyes still looked a little glassy, but otherwise, she was fine. Jeff sent a quick, heartfelt prayer of gratitude heavenward, then shifted his gaze to look over the group of people.

Absently, he noted the sound of sirens as emergency vehicles raced their way.

Jeff frowned and swept the faces of the crowd again, looking for and not finding one particular person.

"Agnes," he muttered. A sinking sensation flared up in the pit of his stomach and slowly unfurled fingers of dread.

"What? What about her?" Laura asked, turning her head to stare at the building behind them.

"She's not here," he said, his voice scraping against his throat. He handed the baby to Laura and started walking toward the apartment house. "She didn't get out."

"Are you sure?" Laura asked, following in his footsteps.

"No," he turned his head this way and that, checking out the faces surrounding him. No, he wasn't sure. She might have gone to a neighbor's, but the neighbors were all here, watching the commotion. "I don't see her anywhere."

Laura's hands gripped the baby tightly. "Oh God, Jeff..."

He had to check. He had to make sure the older woman had made it to safety. Just the thought of Agnes Butler trying to maneuver her way through a burning building alone was enough to get him moving.

"Stay here," he ordered in a tone that had been known to make privates and corporals leap for cover. He paused long enough to stroke her cheek, then he was running. Running toward the open doorway where smoke billowed out into the evening.

Laura watched him disappear into the thick gray fog and kept her gaze locked on the last spot she'd seen him. She couldn't look away. She couldn't draw a breath.

Lord. Standing beside her one minute, he'd been gone in the next. Maybe forever. What if he was overcome by the smoke? What if the fire spread despite the neighbors' efforts? What if the fire department got here too late?

So many risks. So many dangers.

Her heart pounding, she told herself that he was a trained soldier. He would be all right. Her blood chilled. A career Marine. A man schooled in war and battle. A man who could be sent off to fight in some far-off place at any time.

Danger and risk were a part of his life. Death was never too far from a man whose job it was to fight his country's enemies.

Tremors rocked her. How had she allowed herself to become even remotely involved with Jeff? Why hadn't she ever once stopped to think about his being a Marine? A warrior?

Oh God, oh God, oh God... The phrase kept repeating in her brain, over and over like some ancient chant designed to ward off evil spirits. But she knew that frantic prayers and hastily offered deals to the Almighty didn't work. Nothing worked. Nothing could keep him safe if some odd twist of Fate decided that tonight was his night to die.

Oh, *please,* she thought, terrified. Not Jeff. Not now. Not yet. Not yet? her brain screeched. When, then? After they'd lived together and loved together and had more children? Would *then* be the time to lose him? Would the pain be less or more?

Tears stung her eyes. She told herself they were caused by the smoke, but she knew that one for a lie even as she thought it. Fear was the enemy here. Her fears. Her weaknesses. Her body trembled, and her grip on Miranda tightened in response.

She couldn't do this. Couldn't risk it.

Not again. Not ever again.

She didn't realize just how tightly she was holding on to Miranda until the baby squirmed against her uncomfortably. Immediately, Laura loosened her grasp a bit, trying at the same time to fight down her fears. The infant's cries continued to blast into the lavender twilight and seemed to intensify when the emergency trucks pulled up behind them.

In seconds, firemen were streaming across the lawn. Pushing the crowd back to safety, they unreeled their water hoses and took over the task of quelling the fire.

A man, a paramedic she thought, came up to her, wanting to check her and the baby over, but Laura only shook her head. They were fine, she knew. Maybe later, she would let the man examine Miranda, but not now. For now, she had to concentrate her focus and her prayers on that front door.

Jeff, she thought frantically, what's taking him so long? Why wasn't he out yet? Why wasn't he there, beside her?

Old fears rose up and threatened to choke her. Her throat closed up tight, and she had to struggle to breathe. Not again, she prayed. Please don't let the man she loved die. Not again.

She groaned, an aching rumble of fear and pain that came from deep in her soul. She wasn't merely *involved* with the man. It was far worse than that. Dear God, she loved him. Despite her efforts. Despite everything, she loved him. More deeply, more completely than she had ever loved before.

Tears pooled in her eyes as she acknowledged that her feelings for Bill couldn't compare to the depth of the emotions she felt for Jeff.

She doubted anything could.

Swiping one hand across her eyes, she jiggled Miranda on one hip and squinted into the smoky haze filling the entryway of the apartment building. As if she could *will* him to safety, she concentrated on the image of his face and tried to silence the terror building inside her. But it wouldn't be denied its chance to torment her.

Where was he?

Why hadn't he come out yet?

Fear rippled along her spine. Dread echoed in her brain as one word repeated itself over and over. Gone, gone, gone.

Laura choked back a sob. No. She couldn't go through this again, she told herself.

She would never survive the pain.

Laura dragged a deep gulp of air into her lungs and reminded herself that this was why she had hidden for so long. This was why she had decided not to love again. *This* was the agony she'd thought and hoped and prayed to avoid.

To no avail.

Desperate tears stung her eyes as endless seconds ticked by.

Then he was there.

Agnes Butler clutched firmly to his chest. Jeff, his face sooty, stepped through the now thinning haze.

His gaze found hers instantly.

And Laura lived again.

Eleven

It wasn't much of a fire really, more smoke than flame. Someone had allowed the water in a pan to boil away and by the time they'd caught it, their kitchen was filled with smoke, driving them outside.

The quick-thinking neighbors with their garden hoses had pretty much saved the day. A few hours later, the fire department allowed the tenants back into the building.

Adrenaline still pumping through his blood, Jeff stood at the window in the living room while Laura put the baby to bed. He stared out at the neon and what stars he could make out in spite of the reflected lights of the town and tried to calm himself.

Everyone was fine. Nothing tragic had happened. Although, he thought with a brief smile, Agnes Butler might never be the same. She'd been wearing earphones to listen to her stereo and hadn't heard the smoke alarms go off. Jeff still wasn't sure how she had finally heard him pounding on her door, but he'd never forget the look on her face when he'd told her there was a fire in the building.

She'd even submitted to being carried out because, though it had hurt her pride to admit it, she was too slow to make good time.

Idly, he reached up and touched the cheek she had deigned to kiss once he'd carried her to safety. Of course, he realized that her newfound fondness for him probably wouldn't last long.

Inhaling sharply, he set his hands on either side of the window frame and leaned in, resting his forehead on the cool glass pane.

He shouldn't be as churned up inside as he was. Why wasn't he calming down now that the threat to his family was over? Abruptly, he shoved away from the window and started pacing. His footsteps echoed through the room like a thundering heartbeat.

Was the threat gone, though? he wondered. Pushing both hands across the sides of his head, he shot a quick glance at Laura's closed bedroom door. Inside that room were the two most important people in the world to him. And he could have lost them both tonight.

Hell, what was driving him insane was that he could *still* lose Laura. He'd seen the look on her face and recognized it. Shell shock. The same expression he'd seen carved into the features of people who had watched their homes and lives destroyed by war.

People who had given up on life.

The bedroom door opened quietly, and he snapped

his head around. She stood framed in the doorway. Dim light from the corner lamp fell on her, dusting her in a pale ivory glow. His chest tightened as his gaze locked on her shadow-filled brown eyes.

He had the distinct feeling that she was drawing away from him even as they stood there, staring at each other.

Laura had heard him before she'd opened the door. His footsteps quick, almost angry, he'd been pacing the apartment floor like a caged tiger.

If there had been a way to avoid him, she would have. Cowardly or not.

She let her gaze slide from his. Her emotions were still too close to the surface. She didn't want him to be able to see the conflict raging inside her.

"Miranda all right?" he asked, his voice a low growl.

"Yes. She's asleep." Keep the sentences short, she told herself. Don't invite a conversation.

"Good," he said. "Because we have to talk."

"Not now," Laura told him, and rubbed her hands up and down her arms, hoping for some warmth to dispel the chill that seemed to have settled in her bones.

"You can't put this off," he said, starting toward her.

Laura quickly sidestepped, moving for the kitchen. Keep busy, she thought. Make coffee. Do the dishes. *Anything.* "Hasn't there been enough activity for one night?" she asked quietly from over her shoulder.

"No," he said, then paused. "Damn it, Laura," he

continued, following her into the tiny kitchen. "Stand still and listen to me."

She shook her head, refusing to turn around and face him. Looking into his eyes would only make this so much harder.

He wouldn't be put off, though. He stepped up behind her, grabbed her arms and turned her around. Her back pressed to the edge of the counter, she met his blue eyes and saw a flash of emotion that shot a tremor of warning down her spine.

"Laura," he spoke more softly now, his gaze moving over her features like a caress. "What happened tonight scared the hell out of me."

Her heart breaking, she said, "It scared all of us." She would never forget the image of Jeff racing into danger. She *couldn't* forget the mind-numbing minutes she'd spent waiting to see if he'd survived.

"I know you were scared, too." His hands gentled on her arms, and his thumbs moved over the fabric of her nightshirt. "But the fear made me think, too."

"Jeff, don't," she pleaded, even knowing that it was too late. Love shone in his eyes. Determination etched into his features, and she realized there was no way to escape hearing the declaration she knew was coming.

Logically, Laura knew she was being foolish. She should be happy that such a man loved her. But happiness was an ephemeral emotion. And despair stretched on forever.

"I have to say this," he told her. "Tonight made me realize that what we have together is too fragile to be taken for granted." Abruptly, he let her go, took a

half step away from her, then stopped and ran one
hand across the back of his neck. His voice dropped
as if he were speaking to himself, not her, as he continued. "I figured I'd have all summer to convince
you."

No, he wouldn't have, she thought sadly, forcing
herself to keep from reaching for him. She never could
have stayed the whole summer. But he didn't know
that.

"Now I know that I can't take the chance of waiting." He shrugged helplessly. "For all I know, I could
step into the street tomorrow and get run down by a
truck."

Her breath caught. Memories of a long-ago car accident that had shattered her world rose up, and she
relentlessly battled them down again.

He came back to her, cupping her face in his hands,
his fingers spearing into her hair at her temples. "I
don't want to wait another day to tell you that I love
you."

Her eyes filled with tears, and she blinked them
back. What she wouldn't have given in that moment
to be able to tell him that she loved him, too. Three
small words. How could they both warm her and terrify her?

"I know you don't want to hear this," he said in a
rush, apparently sensing her turmoil. "But, Laura,
life's too fragile to not say the things that are important to us."

Panic burned in the pit of her stomach. She knew
very well just how fragile life was. Fragile enough that
to care about anyone as much as she did him was to

leave yourself open to disaster and unbearable pain. She couldn't do that. She couldn't risk everything only to have Fate snatch it away from her again.

"I want you to marry me," he blurted, then stopped and smiled at her. "Man, there's something I never figured to say."

Her eyes widened. Suddenly frightened, she worried that just by his speaking the words out loud, he'd thrown a challenge at the feet of the gods of happiness.

"Don't say anything more," she whispered, and reached up to lay her fingertips across his mouth to silence him, though it was already too late.

He kissed her fingers, then spoke anyway, refusing to be hushed. Her hand dropped to her side.

"I'm going to say it, and you have to listen. I realized tonight that I couldn't take the chance of losing you, Laura." His voice dropped, husky with emotion. "You're to important to me. I can't even imagine living without you." He sucked in a gulp of air. "I thought I could wait. Give you time. But I can't. I need a commitment between us, Laura. I need to be married to you."

She gathered up her remaining strength and said, "Being married isn't a guarantee, Jeff."

He gave her a half smile. "I didn't say I needed guarantees. I just need you."

She needed guarantees. She needed someone to tell her that this time it would be all right. This time, the man she loved would live forever. But since she couldn't have that promise, she wouldn't risk loss again.

She started to speak, but he cut her off.

"Don't answer yet," he said quickly, his gaze boring into hers. "Think about it. Think about us. Miranda." He slid one hand down to cover her flat belly. "You may be pregnant, Laura. Think about that, too."

His eyes closed and he leaned toward her, pressing his brow to hers. "I *love* you, Laura," he whispered. "And I know you love me and Miranda. Neither of us planned for this to happen. But didn't you tell me once about life shattering your plans and how you had to adapt? Accept?"

She nodded stiffly and remembered the eight long, lonely years she'd hidden her heart and soul from the world.

His arms closed around her, pulling her flush against him. "We could be happy together, Laura, the three of us." He kissed the top of her head. "Hell, maybe the *four* of us. But I think you already know that."

Yes, they could be happy. If only the risk weren't so great. As for the chance of her being pregnant, she wouldn't worry about that yet. She still had another week before they would know. Time enough then.

Although, she thought, the idea of Jeff's baby growing inside her was somehow a comforting one.

"Love me, Laura," he said, bending his head to give her a kiss. "And let me love you."

She leaned into him. The instantaneous flash of heat between them warmed her to her soul. Tonight, she thought, giving herself over to the incredible sensations he created in her. They could have this one last night together. They deserved at least that much, didn't they?

She reached up, wrapped her arms around his neck,

and when he lifted her into his arms, she sighed into his mouth. Quickly, he carried her to his bedroom, and in seconds, their clothes were scattered across the rug and they lay entwined in each other's embrace.

His hands seemed to be everywhere at once. Stroking, caressing, his palms moved over her familiarly, rediscovering her body as if for the first time.

Laura arched into him as his mouth closed over her breast. She felt every flick of his tongue as an arrow piercing the coldness wrapped around her heart. He suckled her, and she felt him draw the last of the loneliness from her. Her hands cupped around the back of his head, she held him in place, silently demanding more of him.

He gave. Lavishly, he adored her breasts, one after the other, while his hands moved expertly over her flesh, stoking the kindling in her blood to a raging blaze.

When he moved to slide along the length of her body, Laura moaned softly. His lips and tongue forged a trail across her skin. New patches of desire rippled to the surface as he slowly, deliberately drove her.

Each kiss was a promise. Each caress a blessing.

At last, he moved to take a position between her thighs.

Hungering for the feel of him inside her, Laura lifted her arms to hold him, but he made no move to lie atop her. Instead, he slid his hands under her bottom and lifted her hips from the bed.

"Jeff," she whispered, "what are you doing?"

His eyes glazed with passion, he met her gaze

squarely. "Loving you," he answered, and lowered his head.

She gasped aloud when his mouth came down on her center. Her fingers curled into the sheet beneath her, searching for purchase in a suddenly spiraling world.

His tongue swirled over and around a tiny piece of sensitized flesh. She jerked in his grasp and couldn't quite contain the groan of pleasure that ripped from her throat.

He lifted his head and smiled at her. Moving his hands from her behind, he shifted first one of her legs, then the other, to his shoulders.

She looked at him, caught by the gleam in his eyes. Mesmerized, she continued to stare at him as he slowly, teasingly, covered her with his mouth again. Laura's eyes closed briefly, then flew open again.

Helplessly suspended in air, Laura could do nothing but feel. She watched him take her. Erotic sensations sizzled through her body as he gave her most intimate flesh long, luxurious strokes with his tongue.

Her hips lifted, her heels digging into his back. She swayed unsteadily as his mouth took her to heights she had never dreamed of before.

Then he slipped one finger inside her, and the last of Laura's composure splintered. Too many sensations at once clamored through her brain, demanding to be recognized. Her breath came in short, ragged gasps as her hips lifted into his touch again and again.

The world around her rocked as the first tremors rippled through her. His lips and tongue worked faster now, urging her on. Her eyes slid closed as a final, overpowering surge of pleasure rocketed around inside her.

Jeff set her down gently on the mattress, reached into the nightstand drawer and pulled out the condom he needed so desperately. When he was ready, he pushed himself into her, relishing her soft moan of pleasure.

Fed by an almost frantic desire, he raced toward the completion waiting for him and, with one final thrust, joined her on the other side of passion.

Some time later, Laura stirred from her dreams and turned into Jeff's embrace. He muttered something in his sleep and tightened his grip on her.

Caught halfway between being asleep and being awake, Laura sneaked a peek at the bedside clock—2:00 a.m. The night was almost gone, and they were wasting it in sleep.

She pressed a kiss onto his chest, then shifted her head until she could run her tongue across his flat nipple. He sighed heavily.

A sheen of tears blurred her vision, but she blinked them back determinedly. She wouldn't allow herself to cry. Not now, anyway. There would be plenty of time for tears later. In the months and years she faced without him.

Lifting her head, she looked down at him, memorizing each of his features, etching them into her heart. If things were different, she thought. If she were braver, if he had a less dangerous job, if there were guarantees…

No. No more *if*s. She'd made her decision. It wasn't

an easy one, and God knew she already had regrets. But there was really no other choice. She couldn't face a lifetime of worry. Fear.

She bent her head and kissed the corner of his mouth. His eyes opened to slits. He looked up at her and gave her a grin that would haunt her forever.

This had to be enough, Laura told herself. She would have tonight with Jeff.

Tomorrow, she would leave.

By midmorning the following day, the sky was overcast and dreary. Heavy gray clouds threatened rain but did nothing about it. The weather matched her mood perfectly.

The phone rang just as she was zipping her last suitcase.

Laura straightened up and stared at it. If it was Jeff calling, she didn't want to talk to him. She was afraid he would be able to tell by the tone of her voice that something was wrong. It would be better...easier if he didn't find out about her leaving until the deed was done.

On the other hand, if he decided to come home to find out why she wasn't answering the phone...

Instantly, Laura hurried to the table and snatched the receiver off the hook. "Hello?"

"Hi," Jeff said, his voice low and intimate. "What took you so long?"

"Uh—" she shot a glance at the baby in her stroller "—I was changing Miranda."

"Give her a kiss for me."

"I will," she said, her heart breaking.

"Give one to yourself, too."

Laura's grip on the phone tightened until she was afraid she'd snap the instrument right in half.

"Is everything all right?" he asked.

"Yeah," she answered after clearing her throat. "Everything's fine. Uh, I'm taking Miranda out for a couple of hours." She flinched at the lie. "So if you call, I won't be here."

"No problem," he said. But she heard an undertone of concern in his voice. "Have fun."

"We will," she said, eager now to hang up.

"Laura..."

She bit back a sigh. "Yes?"

"About last night..."

She didn't want to think about last night. She couldn't. Not when she was leaving him.

"Jeff," she told him brusquely, "I've got to go before Miranda starts getting cranky."

"Sure," he agreed quietly. "Go ahead. We can talk later."

"Later." She nodded to herself. Later she would be gone.

"I love you, Laura."

She winced, squeezing her eyes shut. On a sigh, she whispered, "I know."

Laura set the receiver back in its cradle and caressed it absently before turning away. She picked up her purse and the suitcase from the couch and paused to glance at the sealed envelope she'd left on the coffee table for Jeff. Then she pushed Miranda's stroller into the hall, where the rest of her bags were already waiting.

Agnes's door was open, the older woman standing on the threshold, watching her.

"I appreciate you taking care of the baby this afternoon, Agnes," Laura said.

She nodded her gray head and peered at Laura through those sharp blue eyes of hers. "I'll enjoy it," she replied. "Though I think you're makin' a big mistake."

"I can't stay," Laura answered, and closed Jeff's door firmly. Just as she was closing the door on any future she might have had with him. "The new nanny will be here tomorrow." Her bottom lip trembled slightly at the thought of someone else caring for *her* baby, but she had no choice. "I spoke to the head of a very reputable agency a couple of hours ago. She assured me that their nannies are extremely well qualified and that Miranda would be in good hands."

"You're bein' a damn fool," Agnes said quietly.

Laura's gaze snapped to the other woman's.

"Oh, Jeff Ryan's no prize, but he's a good man." She wagged one gnarled finger at Laura. "You should be snappin' him up, not runnin' for cover."

"Agnes, it's just not that simple."

"Love is always simple," the other woman asserted with a slow shake of her head. "It's people who make it hard."

"Life makes it hard," Laura whispered.

"Runnin' doesn't make it any easier," Agnes said, a trace of compassion in her voice. "You'll find that you can't run far enough or fast enough to leave what you feel behind."

The older woman's words echoed in the hollow blackness that had become Laura's heart.

Agnes stepped up closer to her and gave her an awkward pat on the arm. "Why not stick around a bit longer?" she suggested. "Give it another day or so."

Every day she stayed only made it harder to leave. It was now or never.

"I have to go," Laura said. "My plane..."

"Hope you know what you're doin', girl."

"I do," she whispered. The only thing she *could* do.

"One of these days, y'know," Agnes added, "you're going to regret this. A lot."

Laura gave her a watery smile. "That's where you're wrong, Agnes," she said. "I already regret it."

Twelve

Jeff held the huge bouquet of flowers behind his back as he opened the front door. Foolish perhaps, but he wanted to catch the look of pleased surprise on Laura's features when he presented them to her.

"She's not there."

Frowning, he turned around to face Agnes Butler, standing in her open doorway. Sympathy shone in her eyes, and he tried to ignore it. "What? Where'd she go?"

"She's gone."

Amazing the effect that two simple words could have on a man's nervous system. His mouth dry, he managed to croak out a question. "Where?"

"Home, she said."

Home. Apparently *he* had been the only one to consider this place her home, as well as his.

"The baby?" he asked.

"Inside." She nodded toward her own apartment. "Sleeping."

He nodded stiffly. His fingers tightened around the cellophane-wrapped bouquet he still held. The rustling sound seemed to echo around him. Drawing the flowers from behind his back, he smirked down at them. *Surprise.*

"She said she left you a note," Agnes continued.

"A note." He nodded again, congratulating himself on the movement. After the night they'd shared. After his proposal of marriage. She'd left him a note and disappeared.

A hollow emptiness opened up inside him.

Damn it, he'd had a feeling something was wrong. When he'd talked to her earlier on the phone, he'd heard a tremor in her voice that had worried him. But he'd convinced himself that all was well. That they would talk everything out when he got home.

He'd never guessed that she would simply run away.

"Jeff? You all right?"

He glanced at the older woman. Strange that his old nemesis should now feel like his only friend. "I'll be right over to get the baby."

"No hurry," she said. "Take your time."

Jeff stepped into the apartment and closed the door behind him.

Nothingness greeted him. Not one interesting smell from the kitchen. No Miranda gurgling happily in her high chair. No Laura singing softly to herself.

The emptiness in his soul began to slowly fill with anger. How could she just leave, without a word?

Then he remembered. A note.

Grinding his teeth together, he let his gaze shoot around the room. He spotted it almost instantly. A plain white envelope, his name scrawled across it, lay on the coffee table.

A muscle in his jaw ticked. He tossed the bouquet down onto the sofa and grabbed the envelope. Quickly, he tore it open, pulled out the single sheet of paper inside and read it.

Dear Jeff,
The baby is with Agnes, and I've arranged for a new nanny to start working for you tomorrow. I didn't want it to be this way, Jeff, but I can't marry you. Please understand and don't follow me. I'll always remember you and Miranda.

Love, Laura.

"'Love, Laura'?" he asked aloud. "How the hell could she sign a goodbye note 'Love, Laura'?"

And "Please understand"? Understand what? That she had no guts?

Glancing down at the note in his hand, Jeff slowly, thoroughly crumpled it into a ball. "It's not that easy, Laura," he said, fury rising up like bile to choke him. "If you're going to leave me, you're going to have to say it to my face."

Still grumbling, he headed for the phone. Quickly, he dialed Peggy's number. His sister would know where he could find Laura.

On the fifth ring, she answered, clearly out of breath.

"Peggy, it's me," he said shortly.

"Thought I'd be hearing from you," she countered.

"Why?" he asked. "Have you talked to Laura?"

"Yeah. A couple of hours ago."

"She left me, Peg." Lord, those words hit him hard.

Peggy sighed heavily. "I know. I told her I thought it was a mistake."

Jeff pushed one hand across the top of his head and glanced at the crushed roses and daisies lying on his couch. "Why is she doing this?"

"I guess she has her reasons," Peggy evaded nicely.

"Like what?" he demanded, anger pulsing in him. "What could possibly be a good enough reason for her to run away like some damn teenager?"

"Here's a thought," she snapped. "Why don't the two of you talk to each other and stop using me as an interpreter?"

He inhaled sharply. She was right. Any answers he got, he wanted directly from Laura. Damn it, he deserved that much.

"That's why I called you. I need her address."

"Good," Peggy said quickly. "I thought maybe you were going to let her go."

"Not a chance," he whispered, more as a promise to himself than to his sister.

"Got a pencil?" she asked.

He rummaged around for one, then said, "Shoot." After writing down the address, he tore the sheet of paper off the pad and stuffed it into his pocket. "Do you think you could watch Miranda for me while I talk to her?''

"I'd love it," she said, then louder, "Teddy! Put Whiskers down! Cats aren't supposed to fly!"

"I'll call before I come," he said, and then warned, "And while she's there, keep that kid away from my baby.''

"Yeah, yeah. Gotta go," Peggy said, and hung up.

Jeff replaced the receiver and stared blankly into space. It would take him a few days to wrap up some outstanding projects on the base and then to arrange for leave. But by the end of the week, he'd be looking Laura square in the eye, daring her to deny she loved him.

Laura let herself into her apartment and was greeted by voices from the radio she'd left playing while she went to the grocery store. An old song from the sixties streamed into the painfully neat room. She'd unpacked and put all her suitcases away four days ago. Her weary gaze slid around the place she'd called home for eight years. Overstuffed furniture, rag rugs on highly polished wood floors and white lacy curtains fluttering in the breeze drifting under the partially opened windows.

The place used to give her such pleasure. She'd thought it cozy. Homey. Now it just seemed empty. And lonesome. What she wouldn't have given to spy a pacifier lying on the floor. Or that silly pink bunny.

Tears filmed her eyes, and she wiped them away with the back of her hand. She had already cried oceans of tears and found no release from the pain that hammered at her day and night.

She missed him. She missed him so badly it was a constant ache that throbbed in time with her broken heart. Her only consolation was that *this* pain was nothing compared to what she *might* have suffered if she had dared to stay and then lost him.

Slowly, she walked across the room to the kitchen. As she unpacked her grocery bag, she gulped back tears again. No formula. No diapers. Single-serving meals.

And tampons.

Laura's hand dropped to her belly. There was no child nestled there. The proof had arrived only that morning. She should have been relieved, she knew. But strangely enough, she wasn't. Now, not only was she going to have to live without Jeff, but she had also lost her only chance at a family. Children.

She was alone.

Jeff checked the paper in his hand, then marched down the long hallway to the door at the end. He stopped outside her apartment and stared at the closed door in front of him.

Four days without her, and it felt like a damn eternity. What made her think she could just pick up and walk away without a backward glance?

Anger pulsed through him. Damn it, she *loved* him. He knew it. He lifted one hand to knock, then paused, anxiety suddenly wiping away the fury he'd lived with for the past four days.

What would he do if she refused to come back with him?

Jeff's jaw tightened. He bit down on his teeth hard enough to crack them. And with worry still battling hurt and anger, he pounded on her door.

"Who is it?" she called.

He closed his eyes at the sound of her voice. Pain and hunger rose up inside him. It felt like centuries since he'd last seen her. Heard her. Held her.

Breathing deeply, he opened his eyes again and tried to mentally prepare for the fight of his life.

"Laura?" he said in his loudest, made-to-be-heard Marine Corps voice. "It's Jeff. Open this door."

There was a long pause, then she said, "Go away."

"I'm not going anywhere until I say what I came to say," he yelled. Absently, he heard a couple of doors down the hall open up. He glanced to one side quickly and noticed two or three people peeking out of their apartments. He ignored them. "Do you want me to shout it out for everyone to hear? Or are you going to open up?"

He waited what felt like forever, then he saw the doorknob turn. She opened the door and stepped onto the threshold as if her slight body could keep him out.

She looked miserable, and he felt a quick zap of hope blast through him. Purple half circles smudged the flesh beneath her eyes, and her face was pale, giving stark contrast to those shadows. The meadow green, sleeveless summer dress she wore made her skin look even creamier than he remembered.

Jeff's heart staggered painfully. His arms had ached to hold her, and now, suddenly, there she was. Instinctively, he grabbed her, pulled her tightly to him and took her mouth with his. The kiss was long, and hard and deep. Vaguely, he heard her groan and thought he felt her hands slide up his arms before she let them fall to her sides again.

He tasted her tears and inhaled the soft, sweet scent of her, dragging it into his lungs like a drowning man coming up for air for the last time.

Finally, he broke the kiss and released her. She stumbled backward, lifting one hand to cover her kiss-bruised lips.

"You scared the hell out of me," he told her grimly. "Don't *ever* disappear like that again."

"I left you a note," she countered, but her voice sounded high and tight.

"Damn your note," he snapped. "And damn you for making me love you and then leaving."

She blanched, her skin going another shade paler. Nervously, she bent forward, saw the interested faces of their audience and straightened up again. Stepping back into the apartment, she said, "Come inside. Where it's private."

His blood boiling, Jeff marched past her and strode across the room like he was crossing a parade ground. When he reached the opposite wall, he turned around.

As she closed the door and faced him, she asked, "Where's the baby?"

"Do you care?" he nearly shouted.

"Of course I care," she said, and rubbed her eyes with the backs of her hands.

He took a deep breath and exhaled loudly. "She's

with Peggy. I didn't want any interruptions to our 'talk.'"

She nodded stiffly and wrapped her arms around her waist as if for support.

"I would have been here sooner," he told her, "but I have responsibilities. I *can't* just take off anytime I feel like it."

She blinked, but had no defense.

He waited. One minute. Two. When it became obvious that she wasn't going to start the ball rolling, Jeff growled out one word. "Why?"

She swallowed heavily and avoided his gaze.

"You owe me that much at least," he snarled. "Why the hell did you leave? I asked you to marry me, damn it."

"I know," she shouted, and squeezed her middle more tightly. "That's why I left."

He snorted a choked laugh and shook his head. "A simple no would have been enough."

"Would it?" she snapped, taking two hasty steps toward him before stopping short. "Would you really have accepted my refusal?"

He didn't even have to think about that one. "Probably not," he conceded. "But we could have talked about it."

"Talking won't change anything."

"Neither did running away," he said, and had the satisfaction of seeing her flinch from the direct hit.

"Tell me why you're doing this, Laura." Desperately trying to control the wild swirl of emotions churning through him, he struggled to keep his voice even. "Tell me why you're willing to throw us away."

She looked at him then. Her eyes were so pain filled, it hurt him to look at them. He steeled himself against the pang of sympathy he felt for her. Sympathy wouldn't win the day. Only honesty could bridge the gap that had leaped up between them.

A long silent moment ticked past. Finally, though, she shouted, "Because I can't go through this again."

"What?" he demanded.

As if she'd reached her breaking point, the words burst from her lips in a torrent. She told him more about Bill, about his death two weeks before their wedding. About the pain she'd lived with and finally conquered. And about her fear.

"Don't you understand?" she cried, "I love you more than I have ever loved *anyone* in my life! If I lost you like I did Bill, this time the pain would kill me."

"You want guarantees?" he asked.

"Yes, damn it. Promise me. No, swear to me here and now that you won't die. That if we get married we'll live forever!"

"I can't do that."

"Then I can't marry you."

"You're punishing me because Bill died?" Unbelievable.

"I'm not punishing you."

"What is this, then?"

"Self-protection."

"Bull."

"What?" She looked at him like he was speaking some weird foreign language.

"I said that's a load of garbage." Damn it, he

wouldn't lose her to a fear that he had no way of easing. "You're just hiding, Laura. Trying to dig a big enough hole to disappear into."

"You don't know what I went through—" she started to explain.

He cut her off, jumping with both feet into the most important battle of his life. "Another lie." Throwing his hands wide, he shouted right back at her. "I know all about death. I've seen it. Up close and personal. And I know that the most important thing death can teach us is to *live*. Live every moment like it's your last. Squeeze every last damn drop you can out of life. Enjoy every minute for the gift it is."

"You don't understand."

"Yes, I do," he countered. "You're so busy trying not to die, you've forgotten how to live."

She reacted as though he'd slapped her. Drawing her head back, she stared at him through watery eyes.

"I'm not afraid to die," she whispered, her hands at her throat as if choking the words out. "I just don't want to watch *you* die."

"You'd rather watch me walk out of your life?"

"*Yes!* Do it now. *Please.*"

Laura moved back a pace, keeping the distance between them. It was safer that way.

"Trying to hide didn't help, did it?" he demanded. "You didn't want to love me. Or Miranda. But you do."

She looked into those blue eyes of his and couldn't deny the truth. "All right, yes. I do love you. Both of you. But I can't let that love make my choices for me. I *won't* set myself up for that kind of pain again."

"You're crying now," he countered.

Laura lifted one hand to brush across her cheeks.

"What pain have you managed to avoid by leaving me?"

She sniffed and tried to focus on him through the film of water flooding her eyes. "This grief will pass," she told him brokenly. Laura prayed she was right. "But if we become a family and something should happen to you and Miranda..." She shook her head sorrowfully. "That kind of agony would kill me."

Jeff groaned, a tortured sound that erupted from his chest. Closing the space between them, he grabbed her upper arms and gave her a shake. Glaring down into her eyes, he said harshly, "I can't believe you're willing to toss aside something I never thought I'd have."

Her head fell back on her neck. She felt the tension rolling off of him in waves.

"Damn it, Laura, I *love* you. Don't you see what a miracle that is?" He sucked in a gulp of air, held it a moment, then blew it out again, clearly struggling for calm. "Yeah, love is risky. It makes life messy and frightening. Hell, I don't know what will happen tomorrow." His gaze bored into hers, and Laura wept harder at the desperate love she read in his eyes. "I can't give you a guarantee, Laura. I can only tell you that living without love makes for a cold, lonely existence. I know," he said, more softly now.

His hands moved to cup her face. His thumbs brushed her fresh tears away, and she felt the heat of his tenderness reach into the dark corners of her soul and warm them.

"I know what life is without you," he said, "and I

don't want to go back to that. I want to love you. I want to make babies with you.''

Her hand lifted to cover her abdomen.

"Laura?" he asked suddenly. "Are you...?"

"No," she admitted, and felt the emptiness inside threaten to swallow her whole.

He actually looked disappointed, she thought, and when he spoke, he confirmed it.

"I'm sorry. I had been hoping." He shook his head again. "Laura, come with me. Build a family with me."

Jeff. A family.

It was what she had always wanted. Everything inside her screamed at her to throw her fears aside and say yes.

"If only," she whispered, "if only I *knew* everything would be all right this time..."

Jeff bent down and dusted a kiss on her forehead. Love for her filled him so completely that he thought he might burst with it. "Ah, sweetheart," he said tenderly, "I can't promise you that. No one can. The only guarantee I can give you is that I will love you forever." He smoothed her hair back from her face, keeping his gaze locked with hers. "That's all I can say. Our lives are in your hands, Laura."

More scared than he'd ever been on the battlefield, Jeff held his breath and watched her as she looked around her small, quiet apartment.

Laura forced a calming breath into her lungs. Jeff's hands on her face sent ribbons of warmth trailing through her body. Silently, she acknowledged that this was the first time she hadn't been deathly cold since she ran away from him and Miranda. Since she had turned her back on the gift of love. These days without Jeff had been empty. As empty as her life would be if she continued to live scared.

The fear of losing him would probably never disappear completely, she knew. And the prospect of pain was a terrifying one. But, she realized as she turned her gaze back to the face of the man she loved, the reality of living without Jeff Ryan in her life was much more terrifying.

Slowly, she reached up and covered his hands with hers. When she spoke, her voice was hushed. "Eight years ago, I thought my life was over."

He took a breath and held it. Worry lines deepened at the corners of his eyes.

"But it wasn't, Jeff," she said, turning her face into his palm to kiss it. "It's just beginning." She paused and looked into his eyes before saying tenderly, "You are the love of my life. Will you marry me?"

"Yes." A slow, relieved smile curved his lips as he exhaled on a sigh. "I don't mind saying, you had me scared for a while."

"Me, too," she admitted, and moved into his embrace. His arms closed around her, and it felt like a homecoming.

They held on to each other for several minutes, just savoring the joy of being together again.

"Remember," he asked suddenly, "when I told you that I wanted to be the youngest general in the corps?"

She nodded against his chest. His arms tightened protectively around her.

"I've decided to go after a better promotion."

Laura tilted her head back to look at him. "What?"

"To be the best damn husband and father you ever saw."

"You've got my vote, Marine," she said, and went up on her toes to meet his kiss.

* * * * *

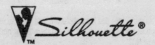

COMING NEXT MONTH

#1177 SLOW TALKIN' TEXAN—Mary Lynn Baxter
Ornery Porter Wyman, November's *Man of the Month,* was married to his Texas fortune, but money couldn't mother his baby boy. Sexy, nurturing Ellen Saxton…now, *she* could raise a child. *And* this single father's desire…for marriage?

#1178 HER HOLIDAY SECRET—Jennifer Greene
Her past twenty-four hours were a total blank! By helping elusive beauty Maggie Fletcher regain her lost day, small-town sheriff Andy Gautier was in danger of losing his *bachelorhood.* But would Maggie's holiday secret prevent her from becoming this lawman's Christmas bride?

#1179 THIRTY-DAY FIANCÉ—Leanne Banks
The Rulebreakers
Tough-as-nails Nick Nolan was lovely Olivia Polnecek's childhood protector. Now *she* was coming to *his* rescue by posing as his fiancée. She'd always dreamed of wearing Nick's ring, sleeping in his arms. So playing "devoted" was easy—and all part of her plan to turn their thirty-day engagement into a thirty-*year* marriage.…

#1180 THE OLDEST LIVING MARRIED VIRGIN—Maureen Child
The Bachelor Battalion
When innocent Donna Candello was caught tangled in Jack Harris's bedsheets, the honorable marine married her in name only. But their compromising position hadn't actually *compromised* Donna Candello at all…and the oldest living married virgin's first wedded task was to convince her new husband to give his blushing bride somethin' to *blush* about!

#1181 THE RE-ENLISTED GROOM—Amy J. Fetzer
Seven years ago levelheaded Maxie Parrish shocked rough-'n'-reckless Sergeant Kyle Hayden, leaving *him* at the altar. And nine months later Maxie had a surprise of her own! Now a certain never-forgotten ex-fiancé appeared at Maxie's ranch rarin' to round up the wife that got away…but what of the daughter he never knew?

#1182 THE FORBIDDEN BRIDE-TO-BE—Kathryn Taylor
Handsome, wealthy Alex Sinclair was Sophie Anders's perfect marriage match. Problem was, she already had a fiancé—his brother! True, her engagement was a phony, but the baby she was carrying was for real—and belonged to Alex. Once Sophie began to "show," would Alex make their forbidden affair into a wedded forever after?